I0684853

Atkinson's Armageddon

The Reaper Series
Book Two

John Paul Bernett

ATKINSON'S ARMAGEDDON

Published by John Paul Bernett.
Cover design V-Edition Media
Author photograph John Orange Photography, Leeds
ISBN: 978-0-9926173-0-1

Dedication

As with all my writing, I dedicate this book to my wife and muse Beverly Bernett. Also my children Gavin, Louise and Hunter. These are the people who make my life whole.

ATKINSON'S ARMAGEDDON

Acknowledgements

Thanks to Beverly Gail Bernett for typing and editing this book. Also to Gavin Johnson and Lee Coates at V-Edition Media for a great cover design. Thanks too to John Orange of John Orange Photography for the author photograph.

.

ATKINSON'S ARMAGEDDON

Foreword

It is well-documented that the last time Armageddon struck this planet, it was the work of a piece of rock from space hitting the Earth. This small piece of rock brought to an end the rule of the dinosaurs, plunging the planet into hundreds of years of darkness that the sun could not penetrate. This has always been thought of as a natural global disaster, and to a degree it was, because Atkinson and Dewhirst have been stepping in and out of the natural world since time immemorial. Coincidentally, the last time these two Gods fought was some sixty-five million years ago. In one of their opinions, the dinosaurs were not worth saving...is Humanity?

We shall see...

JOHN PAUL BERNETT

Prologue

year had passed, and the thoughts of that terrible night were on everybody's minds. One year ago, that very evening, the Earth had faltered and was nearly destroyed. None of the sciences had found out what had happened that fateful evening, although many non-scientific survivors had come up with their own ridiculous theories. Theories such as invisible alien attacks, government conspiracies...even Gods wielding huge swords in the middle of a town in England. The fact was, no one had an answer for what had happened or, for some reason, they were keeping tight-lipped. The only certainty was the epicentre of the devastation was a town in Northern England.

Chapter One

hief Inspector Paul Johnson looked out of the window of his new office in the almost-rebuilt police station at an eerie townscape. There were tower cranes in every direction. The prefabricated buildings with their stark newness housing the city's survivors looked awkward in the new landscape of the distant volcano that rose from the ground the previous year. Much debate had gone into whether new building should take place at all.

To a lot of the townsfolk, the sight of the unblemished oldest building in town seemed to give them the motivation to carry on. This was something that Chief Inspector Johnson found somewhat ironic, as this was the building of Atkinson, Dewhirst & Smith, the local accountancy firm.

The past year had not been a good one for the new Chief Inspector. Looting and lawlessness made up most of the first quarter, with the decimated police force being grossly outnumbered. It was the same at the hospital and the fire station – all public services had been stretched to their limit.

This had not been a localised disaster, this had been worldwide. The after-effects of the battle were not a swift victory for Humankind following the 'War' that took place between the two Gods, Atkinson Junior, Tamara, Sarah and Smith.

With the short 'Famine' that followed, and the 'Pestilence' that set in with the flies and rats on the dead bodies, 'Death' had rode his pale horse and wielded his scythe. You would think Armageddon came, but somehow there were survivors. Armageddon was merely halted In the biblical sense, the Four Horsemen rode out, but the beast that followed had been slain.

Although it couldn't be said that things were now getting back to how they had been, they were surely improving. The gas and water companies were back in business, but both still had many checks to perform before they could say all of their pipelines were safe. The power plant outside of town was back in full swing after receiving minor structural damage. It had however had many system checks from British Nuclear Fuels before the go-ahead to resume supplying power back to the city was approved.

On the outskirts of town were the mass graves, the final resting places of thousands of children, women and men. At least they had been put to rest, albeit en mass...still better than the thousands that were never found.

It was to the outskirts of town that Chief Inspector Johnson was visiting that day, with a single red rose for his fallen comrade Donna Lambert.

While he was at the mass grave, his thoughts turned once again to the battle he had witnessed and survived a year ago. With a pained expression on his face, he knelt down and gently placed the rose at the edge of the solemn grounds where no birds sang and animals stayed away from. Standing up, his thoughts turned to the future. Although he had a good relationship with the accountants at Atkinson, Dewhirst & Smith, the knowledge of who they were and what they did was laying very heavy on his mind.

The hospital was still a building site, but the prefabricated area was as busy as it had been all year – only a more normal service had now resumed. At the hospital's west wing stood the new mortuary with two men inside. Gavin Jackson and Tom Harper were mid-autopsy when the main door burst open, and a very excited Sarah ran in with the top of her arm covered in cling film.

"My arm is finished!" shouted Sarah.

"So is this lovely peace and quiet," replied Tom.

Gavin looked at Tom and smiled.

"I think today is Tuesday, and the reason you are not here and this is a somewhat normal place of work is because you are actually at college!" said Tom.

"Now, now, you two, let's be nice. While Tom and I finish up, you can put the kettle on," said the usual referee.

As Gavin and Tom washed their hands, Sarah made the tea. Tom made his way to the sofa in the lounge, picked up a copy of the Lancet, and began to read. Gavin limped back to his office and began reading through papers that needed to be signed. Sarah finished making the tea and took Tom's beverage to him, which by the smile on his face he was ready for. Sarah giggled and said, "I hope you enjoy it, Tommy."

"My name is Tom, not Tommy," grimaced the lab technician. Once again, Sarah giggled and ran back to the tea station. She placed Gavin's china cup and saucer on a tray along with her Spongebob mug, and walked to Gavin's office. In her usual way, she turned round and opened the door to the office with her bum.

"What a grand entrance you always make, Sarah," said Gavin with a smile on his face.

"I noticed you were limping badly today," said Sarah.

"Yes, it got worse after I dropped you off at college," said Gavin.

"I will give you a rub when we get home," comforted Sarah. "It doesn't seem a year ago that you rode that motorbike into Atkinson's back. We would have lost the battle had you not done that," continued Sarah.

"You amaze me how you are these two different women – the loveable Sarah and this Wonder Woman-type thing. How do you manage it?" asked Gavin.

"Well, unlike Wonder Woman, I wear my knickers underneath my clothes," said Sarah with a grin.

Gavin laughed at her marvellous complexity and then said, "The wedding is getting closer, are you still looking forward to it?"

"More than ever! I'm going to the dressmakers at the weekend to see how my creation is coming along!" said an excited Sarah. "And you won't see it until I'm skipping down the aisle in it!" she continued.

This was of course worrying for Gavin, as he knew morning suits and Ascot hats would be the order of the day for the men and women from his side of the family. He also knew that Sarah's half of the church would be a weird and wonderful assortment of her friends, as she no longer had contact with any of her family.

Gavin was no longer the confident, Jaguar-driving 'young gun' that arrived on a murder scene with the late Chief Inspector Jack Thompson on that dark morning in mid-December 1999. The events of the run-up to the millennium challenged his whole outlook, and his education. The heroic leap on the motorbike twelve months earlier broke his lower right leg in many places. This had left him with a bad limp, but the physical part was easier for him to deal with than the mental part of what had happened. The coroner sipped his tea, and continued his conversation with his betrothed.

"My best friend Hugo Thornton-Ellis has accepted the invitation to be my best man," stated Gavin.

Sarah put her hand to her mouth and started giggling.

"Whatever is the matter? Why are you laughing?" giggled Gavin.

"Well, that's a bit of a mouthful!" laughed Sarah.

"What is?" asked Gavin.

"Hugo...thingy thingy," said Sarah.

"Now, Sarah, he is my best friend, and you mustn't make fun of his silly na...ahem...his name. Anyway, I believe my mother has invited half the county to the wedding," he continued.

"My friends have all sent back the RSVP thingies, and they've all said yes!" exclaimed Sarah.

"I can't wait to see mother's face when they show up, it will be the photograph of the day," said Gavin with a smile.

"I have told them all to wear their best outfits," said Sarah.

"Yes, that's what I am worrying about," answered Gavin.

The conversation was interrupted by Tom knocking on the door and telling Gavin he had a visitor.

"It's okay, I've got to get back to college now, Tommy!" said Sarah, as she gave Gavin a big kiss and said goodbye.

Tom just growled at her and said "Try learning something while you're there and not just another way to make my working life more of a nightmare!"

Sarah skipped by him shouting, "Tommy! Tommy! Tommyyy!" Tom looked at Gavin and with a wry smile on his face and shook his head.

Gavin laughed and said, "Show them in."

"It's okay, there isn't anyone...I had seen the time, and didn't want Madame to be late for her class. She didn't even notice there wasn't anyone here!" laughed Tom.

"Thank you Tom. I would stay here the whole day talking to her, I hadn't noticed the time," said Gavin. The two men resumed the work they were doing before lunch.

Tamara had just finished the list for John Smith's night shift. He had become very proficient at his new line of work; the past year had seen him grow in stature, as everyone outside his building had hit rock bottom at some stage or another. The result of the devastation had not affected the work of Atkinson, Dewhirst & Smith as it had others, with the exception of the first month; John had been very busy, with multiple cords to be severed at the same time. This carried on all the way through that first month, but as medicines and vaccines began to filter through, the workload dropped dramatically.

John Smith looked at Tamara, and said, "It's been an eventful year."

Tamara knew John was reading her thoughts.

"You are in my head again, Atkinson was always doing that."

"Do you still miss him?" asked John.

"The bastard tried to kill me, what do you think?! Anyway, that's all history now...I've got more pressing things on my mind, and you should have, too."

"I do...it's something that has been bothering me all day," said John Smith.

"I thought so. I think today is the day," answered Tamara.

"Well, it has been a year since we heard from them...maybe they've killed each other," said John.

"You have to come to terms with this whole 'immortal' thing, John. We will hear from them today," informed Tamara.

No sooner were the words out of her mouth when both their phones rang simultaneously, and they were transported to the Other Realm.

"Listmaker...Reaper," a long pause ensued and then Atkinson continued. "You averted the end of all things twelve months ago."

"Uhhh, well..."

"Silence, Smith!" screamed Atkinson. "What if it was my creation, and something I wanted to happen?!" he snarled.

"Then it would have happened, Great Lord," grovelled Tamara.

"Indeed it would, but know you this, Listmaker – their efforts have only bought them a little more time. If things don't radically change, I will give them a change they will not live to see. What of my son, Listmaker?"

"My Lord, he's been dissected into seven parts, and placed within the separate realms. One of which being the Plane of Existence.

The whereabouts of the last piece is unknown to you, for your protection," said Tamara with her head bowed.

"Hmmm...and is this place known to you, Listmaker?" demanded Atkinson.

"No, it is not!" interrupted John Smith.

"Silence! You have not proven worthy of addressing me! Be gone!" shouted an enraged Atkinson. Both Tamara and John found themselves back in the office.

"Well, that went well..." observed John.

"Do you have any idea how close you came to losing your head just then? You must learn to bow your head when speaking to them! Only answer a direct question!" informed Tamara.

"I thought I did," quipped Smith.

"The question wasn't aimed at you, therefore, you interrupted him. That, one day, will be a fatal mistake! So only speak when you are spoken to! The only reason you still live is because neither of them have rested enough after the obvious battle that had ensued in that realm! I have it on good authority from one of Mr. Braithwaite's elementals that Atkinson actually lost his head during the fight," informed Tamara.

"You mean...Dewhirst cut his head clean off?

"Indeed he did, but as you just saw, he is ok now, so watch yourself," said Tamara.

John Smith puzzled on how you could lose your head but still live.

"Your life force is separate from your body, we can rejuvenate our bodies at any time, as you saw with me after the fight on the Town Hall clock tower. If you lose your life force; I'm afraid it's game over," said Tamara.

John Smith took on board what she said, and marvelled at the strange life he now lived.

In the Other Realm, the two Gods sat and looked at each other.

"What are your intentions, Atkinson?" said Dewhirst.

"These beings vex me greatly with their endless lust for power and greed. Why should they be spared to bring an end to the world when I can save the world by ending them?"

"You clearly know that it is a minority of people who are causing the problems with their greed and politics," said Dewhirst.

"And why do you care? They are just numbers on a list to you!" sneered Atkinson.

"Your son has been killed and cut into seven pieces, all because he thought like you are doing now! We keep a balance, and that's all! The world you are so fond of saving we nearly destroyed last year with our slight disagreement, and I for one am glad those two were there," answered Dewhirst.

With that, the two deities surveyed their domain. The elementals, whose sole purpose for existence was to take care of the two Gods, were still hard at work repairing their realm after the battle some twelve months past. As for Atkinson and Dewhirst's injuries incurred in that battle, all had healed very quickly – severed limbs re-spawned, and a normal service had resumed.

"So Dewhirst, what of the outcome do you see? After all, your vision is greater than mine," hissed Atkinson.

"What you and your idiot son began last year has yet to finish. You are unconvinced of the human spirit to survive," answered Dewhirst.

"They are no better than the slime they crawled out from," quipped Atkinson.

"I already know of the army you are amassing to retrieve your dismembered son from the Plane of Existence," informed Dewhirst.

"You know nothing!" screamed Atkinson.

"I know this, it's your intention to remove me with the help of your son!" stated Dewhirst resolutely.

"My son is dead!" raged Atkinson.

"He was dead before, but that didn't seem to halt his progress towards the destruction of the Earth!" said Dewhirst.

"This conversation is over!" shouted Atkinson.

"This partnership will soon be over, mark my wordsss," said Dewhirst in a tone Atkinson had never heard before.

"I can end it now!" screamed Atkinson.

"You deranged old fool...you can't end it...I can't end it...but our replacements can," said Dewhirst quite calmly.

"Only you and I can have that set into motion, and as it would mean the end for us both, I can't see that happening – can you?" said Atkinson with a knowing grin.

Dewhirst just smiled at him, but the look of defiance in his eyes worried Atkinson.

Donald Steele was sitting in his makeshift office shouting orders into his phone when Jeff Clarke wandered past his porta-cabin window. Spitting his cigar out of his mouth, he shouted "Clarke! My office! Now! It's been a year, and still no 'story of stories' like I was promised!"

Jeff just smiled as he walked past on his way to see Cindy in the canteen trailer.

"Hi, Cindy," said Jeff, as he entered the canteen. "Fancy having a cuppa with me?"

"It's my coffee break, so the answer is yes!" said his lovely girlfriend.

"I think it's time to do some shopping. We received our invitations to the wedding a while back, and I wondered if you fancied going into town this afternoon to look at dresses and something for me," asked Jeff.

"I finish at 2 pm, I would love to!" answered Cindy.

The couple chatted for a while, and then Cindy went back to work. Jeff stepped out of the canteen and made his way back to the news room, which was now back in full swing, albeit in a prefabricated building.

"The editor was looking for you a few minutes ago, and he wasn't looking too pleased," said Jake Collins, the newsroom supervisor.

"I know, I'm going to see him now," replied Jeff.

The tapping on Donald Steele's office door was received with a "Go Away!" Jeff again smiled and walked in.

"You wanted to see me?" he enquired.

"I will see you on the dole!" retorted Steele. "I'm not paying you to drink coffee in the canteen with that Sally woman!" he continued.

"Cindy."

"What?"

"Her name is Cindy," instructed Jeff.

"I don't care! As good as a cup of tea that she makes is, she's hardly newsworthy! You've never seen a headline that says 'Tea-lady makes tea', Have you!?" growled Steele. "You should be out grabbing headlines, not young women that work in the canteen! Just you be thankful that I'm in a good mood, or you would have been fired! By the way, your review of the anniversary made the front page...but only because there has been no other news today. Don't go around thinking you're a front-page man now, because you're not! Now get out there and bring me some news!" he continued.

Just then, there was another little tap on the editor's door. "Go Away!" was the reply. A muffled scream and the sound of papers hitting the floor could be heard from the other side of the door. Jeff opened the door, to find the editor's new personal assistant on all fours, picking up her papers and sobbing. She came into the office and gingerly placed the work in Steele's 'IN' tray.

"Thank you!" shouted Steele. The girl ran out crying.

"What's wrong with people today? That woman's been here for three weeks, and all I've heard has been crying and sobbing!" complained the editor.

"I can't imagine why that once perfectly-normal woman is now a nervous wreck," answered Jeff.

Chapter Two

Tamara had compiled that night's list, and was handing it to Smith when she paused and looked straight into his eyes and said, "I'm really sorry for being sharp with you when we got back. That time, I was out of place using that tone with you. I'm having trouble adjusting. Atkinson, Dewhirst and Atkinson Jr. did the job differently from you. They took charge, where you don't. You just accept my list and go do your thing – you don't check it or ask questions. Why?"

"Have you ever made a mistake?" asked John Smith.

"I have never made a mistake, and I never will." said a confident Tamara.

"Then why should I check the list, or ask questions about it? I don't know anyone more proficient or professional than you at what you do," answered the Reaper.

"Thank you, John. You don't know how wonderful it is to hear such words," said Tamara.

John Smith's thoughts turned to the earlier audience with Atkinson and Dewhirst.

"What do you think was happening between the two of them?" asked John.

"Something like this has only happened once before, and it was before Atkinson Junior existed. Sixty-five million years ago, give or take a million..." informed Tamara.

"Ahh, the rock from space that killed the dinosaurs?" interrupted John.

"Yes, that rock or asteroid, whatever it was, was not going to hit the Earth until Atkinson changed its trajectory," answered Tamara.

"Atkinson wields that kind of power?"

"Obviously, Atkinson is not his real name, nor is Dewhirst's. They are just names that look good on a balance sheet in an accountancy firm. Those two are Gods, they both sat on Mount Olympus. They wield powers beyond human thought and when they get angry, worlds can end. The people out there have no idea just how close they came last year to the end of all Humankind. It is our job to keep them happy, and to be honest, killing one of their sons and revealing the other's daughter wasn't the best way to keep them at ease," said Tamara.

"Would Atkinson have let his son carry out his plan?" asked John.

"Yes," was the one-syllable reply. "The whereabouts of his son's body parts must be kept from Atkinson, because before he tries another way of killing off the human race, he will want his son back," continued Tamara.

"What? He is going to want him back? To what end?" asked John.

Tamara just lifted an eyebrow and gave the Reaper a knowing glance. "Let's just try and make them a bit happier by doing our jobs well, John, and maybe in a thousand years or so they will settle down to do their work," said Tamara.

"Amen to that!" replied Smith.

Chief Inspector Paul Johnson was now back in his office. The phone was ringing, and there was knocking on his door. He just sat there, taking no notice of what was happening around him. He felt utterly alone, and the pressure of the past year was burgeoning in his mind. The life of a police officer is built on fact and evidence underlining that fact.

The things that he had witnessed had nothing to do with fact or evidence, but they were still there, and they were going around and around in his head. It had been like this for Paul Johnson from the day after the event, when the sun rose on a bleak new landscape.

Having to deal with the survivors...the endless questions of what had happened. His head was full of the deaths of his fellow officers, and friends. The looting...the riots...and more endless death, all of which he had to deal with. Most of all, he was one of a handful of people who knew that Death lived in his own town masquerading as an accountant. Johnson could take no more. His eyes were tired and red, his hand was tightly holding the handle of his service pistol, its barrel resting on his temple. His right index finger began to squeeze ever-so-gently against the steel trigger. He closed his eyes and thought back to happier days.

"You do realize your cord will still be intact when you pull that trigger?" said a gentle, calm voice at his side.

"What?" said Johnson, as the gun was taken from him. As the Chief Inspector's head spun to the side, he saw the beautiful sight of Tamara, with his gun swinging loosely on the extended middle finger of her left hand. She was translucent, with a glow emanating from her. The Chief Inspector's mouth opened as he stared at this Venus de Milo at his side. Tamara smiled at him and said, "John will be here in a minute." Then, the vision disappeared, and the gun fell to the ground just as John Smith entered the office, the locked door not being a problem to him. Smith walked to the side of Johnson's desk, picked up the Chief Inspector's firearm, and sat down in the chair opposite him.

"This is not the way, Paul," said Smith.

"What do you care? I was saving you a bit of work," said Johnson dully.

"No, Paul! You were messing with our book work!" answered the Reaper.

"How much more of this do I have to endure? There is no one else in my position that has to deal with phantoms in their office, not to mention the Grim Reaper calling in for a chat!" said Johnson with his head hanging down.

"And that is the very reason your termination was stopped. Your work is not finished. Your number is still running," said Smith.

"My number is still running? Who am I talking to, the Reaper, or the accountant?" said Johnson.

"I am one and the same, but at the moment, you are talking to your friend John. You need a break, and it just so happens that my firm of accountants have a gift for you. As thanks for your heroic efforts in saving our company last year, we have paid for a holiday for you," said Smith.

"A holiday!? And how am I to go on a holiday? Who will take care of all of this?" asked Johnson.

"Who would have taken care of it had I decided to let you die?"

Johnson just looked up at him and said, "A holiday will do precisely what for me?"

"You will see when you get there," replied Smith.

At that point, police officer Linda Harper, who had been knocking on the door, was let in by John Smith.

"Your tickets have arrived sir, and Detective Inspector Harry Scrivens is downstairs, awaiting your instructions," announced Police Officer Linda Harper.

Chief Inspector Paul Johnson looked at John Smith, and said, "How the hell have you arranged all this?"

A slightly-embarrassed Linda Harper asked her superior who he was talking to.

"Who am I talking to? I am talking to this man! Are you blind, Harper?" said Johnson, as he looked at the empty space that John Smith had occupied only a moment earlier. "Sorry Officer Harper, I was thinking aloud about something else. I think I need this holiday. Can you send D.I. Scrivens up? I have a lot to go through with him."

As she left the office, Police Officer Harper looked confused, and didn't know quite what was going on.

As Chief Inspector Johnson and Detective Inspector Scrivens worked their way through the handover that was going to give Johnson three weeks' leave, in the back of his head, Johnson was thinking he was being railroaded, but was powerless to do anything about it....*So...he might as well just enjoy it...or at least, go along with it.*

He hadn't had any time off during the previous twelve months and he did need a break. Somehow, he knew he could trust Scrivens, and that he was a good man and a good copper – a combination that was getting harder to find in these desperate times. Scrivens was sensible, and did things by the book. There was no gut instinct or working on a hunch with him, it was all matter-of-fact and hard evidence. He had worked his way up through the ranks, and was respected at every rank he had held. *Yes, D.I. Scrivens was definitely a good man to leave in his stead.* What Johnson couldn't work out was how did he know all this because until police officer Harper had said Scrivens was downstairs, Johnson had never heard of him.

Chief Inspector Johnson put on his jacket and made his way to the front desk, where Glenn Simpson, the desk sergeant, was up to his elbows in lost cats, missing garden gnomes and the women at No. 31 getting undressed with the curtains open.

Chief Inspector Paul Johnson just walked by and said, "If anybody wants me, let Scrivens deal with it. See you all in three weeks." With those few words, the Chief Inspector was gone.

On entering his car, he suddenly thought, *where am I going?* He took out the tickets from his inside jacket pocket to peruse their contents. As Johnson was musing over his tickets, he decided to call in on John Smith and Tamara. Parking his car in the alley at the side of the old building, he walked around to the front door.

"Good morning, Chief Inspector. I will let Mr. Smith know you are here."

"Thank you," said Johnson.

"Come this way," invited Mr. Braithwaite.

"Paul! Nice to see you on this plane!" said Smith.

"Yes...well...all of these different planes are driving me mad!"

"Come, take a seat. Would you like some tea?" enquired John Smith.

"I think I need a strong coffee. What just happened to me in my office? One minute I was about to end it all, the next you two are there, but not really, and then I'm going on holiday!" replied Johnson.

"You simply need to take a break, that's all," said Tamara.

"Let me put it this way, Paul – we need things to get back to normal, and a new Chief Inspector might look too deeply into what happened last year," said Smith.

"Do you think a holiday will help me?" asked Johnson.

"Yes!" replied Tamara and Smith simultaneously.

"Whether you like it or not, you know what we do here, so that means to protect ourselves, we must protect you. The status quo must carry on," said Tamara.

"This break will really work, Paul," said John Smith.

With that, the Chief Inspector drank the rest of his coffee and made for the door.

"The car is waiting for you, with your luggage, outside the front door. We will make sure yours finds its way back to the police station. See you after your cruise!" waved Tamara.

"See you in three weeks," said the slightly confused Chief Inspector.

"That was a close thing," said Tamara.

"Why did we just do that, Tamara?" asked John.

"It is like how I explained it to the Chief Inspector, John. What we need is for there to be calm. Calm on all levels – here, and in the Other Realm. Atkinson and Dewhirst are still against each other, and either of them can do their space-rock manoeuvre, and then it's all over. Death will be instantaneous for some, a long freezing for others. They did it before, and if provoked enough, they will do it again. In my opinion, if Chief Inspector Johnson or Gavin Jackson were replaced, their successors would go through their files...and we have no idea what is in those files," answered Tamara.

"Let's just remove their files," said John.

"We are not allowed to interfere," said Tamara.

"Haven't we just interfered, stopping Johnson from killing himself?"

"We didn't interfere, as such...we were just there at the time when he needed someone to talk to," answered Tamara.

"Tamara, you were in the Other Realm," said John.

"You're just splitting hairs! It was all a coincidence!" replied Tamara, with that little smile John had become accustomed to.

The drive in the back of the limousine was both relaxing and enjoyable, as the Chief Inspector was listening to his favourite music and was served lunch by a beautiful young woman who was in the vehicle when he boarded at Atkinson, Dewhirst & Smith.

"Is that to your liking, Chief Inspector?" smiled the young woman.

"It's my absolute favourite meal! How could you know I love fry-up...and furthermore how do you make fry-up without the remnants of Sunday dinner?" asked Johnson.

The woman just enigmatically smiled and poured the Chief a glass of beer.

Paul Johnson began to think maybe he had squeezed that trigger, and this was the afterlife.

"No, it isn't, Sir," said the driver.

"It isn't what?" inquired the Chief Inspector.

"The afterlife, Sir," answered the driver.

Amazed at what the chauffer had just said, he replied, "You can read my thoughts?"

"Yes, Sir," answered the driver. "To answer your other questions – we are here to help you, we work for the accountancy company, I am to be your valet, and the girl at your side is to be your travelling companion."

"Will we be talking at all during this holiday?" asked Johnson.

"Yes, Sir," said the drive with a smile.

Chief Inspector Paul Johnson sat back, and the soft leather made that distinctive squeaking noise that it alone makes.

"Is the rest of my holiday going to be in the style of this car?"

"Indeed it is, Mr. Johnson, for the next three weeks, you are no longer a policeman," instructed his travelling companion.

Mr. Paul Johnson placed his hands behind his head and said, "That will do nicely."

Outside the college, Gavin Jackson was listening to Beethoven's 9th symphony with his eyes closed, not thinking about work, he was just in his 'happy place'. All of a sudden, the car door burst open. With the swish of a tartan miniskirt and a flash of pink knickers, Sarah launched herself into the passenger seat, still with Clingfilm around her arm, his peace totally destroyed.

"Hello darling! Did you miss me? Have a listen to this...I borrowed it from my friend Sophie!" She immediately took out the CD that was playing and replaced it with Marilyn Manson's 'Disposable Teens'. To say that Gavin nearly jumped out of the car was an understatement. When he regained his senses, he said, "Hello, my dear, how was college? And what has happened to the car's sound system?"

"It's Marilyn Manson's new song, don't you love it?" enthused Sarah.

"She has a very masculine voice," replied Gavin.

"It's a guy, silly! It's better than listening to your morgue music!" said Sarah as she planted a kiss on his lips. As Gavin's car pulled away, he thought...*morgue music? Ludwig would be spinning in his grave!*

The trip back for Sarah was wildly exciting, but sheer torture for her betrothed. But as ever, he bore his discomfort with grace and a smile, because although his girl was the strangest person he had ever met, she was the only one who made his heart race. It wasn't long before they were home, and home was now a two-bedroom cottage in a small village about 45 minutes from the town centre by car.

The car pulled into the bare beech tree-lined lane that led to the picture-postcard English cottage. Half of the building was covered in ivy, and the garden was full of roses – and during summertime, they were magnificent – but as it was winter, they looked quite sad. It was, in fact, his parents' cottage which they used if ever they were in Yorkshire.   But as soon as the devastation of the previous year hit, within a couple of days they had persuaded their son to move to it. It was in fact not until six weeks later that the move took place, because Gavin was in hospital, and Sarah was in the Other Realm recovering from the battle. Both Sarah and Tamara spent time recouping and getting to know each other, whilst John Smith stayed back on the Plane of Existence and the Realm of Death. Tamara had been sending lists constantly for the first week she was there to cover the mass deaths for the Reaper to deal with.

On exiting the vehicle, Gavin, as ever, helped Sarah from the car and the couple made their way to the door. The entrance led straight into the living room, which was fourteen feet by twelve feet in size. It had a large original Range fireplace and oak beams on the ceiling. The walls were decorated with wallpaper adorned with small pink roses. The three-piece suite was an oxblood leather Chesterfield. Oh yes, this was definitely his parents' cottage – it wasn't his style at all, but for the moment, he was glad it was at their disposal.

"I'll put the kettle on," offered Sarah.

"I'll start the dinner," replied Gavin.

They had called in at the local shops for their groceries on the way home. Although this wasn't his chosen way of shopping, as he preferred to get everything at a supermarket, he was in fact enjoying shopping the old-fashioned way. He knew, however, it wasn't going to be for long. His parents were planning something special for a wedding present. On their last visit to the family home, while Sarah was playing on his old swing in the garden with the chambermaid, his mother asked him for advice on things like apartments, modern conveniences, and how he would decorate said apartment. She said she was thinking of buying one for herself and his father for when they went to town. He remembered thinking it must be five years since mother had even been to their local town centre, never mind buying an apartment there.

His daydreaming came to an end when Sarah placed his tea in front of his face, and said, "Tea up!"

"Thank you, Sarah. Could you pass me the pan for these potatoes?"

"One spud-pan coming up!" replied Sarah.

The lamb chops were roasting in the oven, the potatoes, peas and carrots boiling on the stove, and the soon-to-be-wed couple sat down on the couch to drink their tea.

"Sarah," said Gavin. "I've been meaning to ask, when you were in the Other Realm with Tamara after the battle, what did you do?"

"Are you sure you want to know? Because, you haven't wanted to talk about it before..." said Sarah.

"I know, and I'm sorry about that. It was just that most of what I had been taught was rubbished on that day. I couldn't understand how it could be happening. The whole thing made me mistrust my entire way of thinking. But I have to live with that, and I need to move on, so it's time for me to embrace the other Sarah."

Sarah sat sideways on the couch, looking straight at him. She crossed her legs, put her elbows on her knees, and with her chin resting in her hands she said, "Well, it turns out that I have lived many, many lives. I have lived, and died, many times over the centuries. I was sired by a God, as was Tamara – but the God who was my father didn't trust his partner, so to keep me from his knowledge, he made me live life as a human until the day I would be needed...and that was last year. I am still Slabgirl, but I am a protection guardian as well. I like both sides of me...and I hope you will too."

"Do I rethink my way of life? Should I change my way of thinking, and learn more about this?" asked Gavin.

"No. There are but a few humans who know of our existence so when you, the Chief Inspector and Jeff die, once again no one will know of us and everything will be as it was," explained Sarah.

"Does this mean we have to worry about having a short life?" asked Gavin.

"Not at all! You guys will prove very useful to John and Tamara."

"How do you mean?" asked Gavin.

"I don't know, that just came into my head, and I don't know why I said it," said a puzzled Sarah. "Maybe this thing isn't over – I feel strange. Can we stop talking about it now, my love?"

"Of course darling. I'm sorry I asked too many questions," comforted Gavin.

The timer on the oven sounded. "Ah, time for dinner," said Gavin.

All through dinner Sarah was pensive and wore a worried expression. "A penny for them?" offered Gavin.

Sarah smiled sweetly and said, "It's just something Tamara said while I was in the Other Realm with her. She said we will have to protect the humans who were involved because their part in all of this may not be coincidental. What do you think she means?"

"Who knows? Maybe I might be wearing my underpants on the outside of my trousers, too!" laughed the coroner.

That made Sarah laugh and distracted her thoughts away from the subject. Although Gavin was laughing along with her, he was thinking about the unthinkable...of going through all of what they went through for a third time.

"That's enough of the other Sarah – let this one see to that hurting leg of yours. Come on upstairs in a minute, and I'll get the oils ready," said Sarah.

When Gavin limped upstairs, the candles were all burning and the lights had been dimmed. Sarah was standing naked with the prepared oils in her hands, ready to bestow upon him her holistic pleasures. She helped him undress, and Gavin laid on the bed.

Sarah knelt on the bed beside his now-crooked leg, and gently placed warm oil upon it. Her hands on his leg felt wonderful, and Gavin let out a sigh, followed by a moan of pleasure. Sarah knew exactly where to massage, and her soft, loving hands were doing the job as if she were an old master.

This was yet another side of the girl who, when he first saw her, lived up to the nickname of 'Slabgirl' – in fact, he wondered how it was possible to fall in love so quickly with someone he would have never even dated. Up until meeting Sarah he had only dated socialites...perhaps Destiny was playing a hand in this coming together. But for now, he cared not of Destiny, he just knew that she was perfect and everything he could want in life. Gavin emerged from his thoughtful state as Sarah's hands moved to his back. She was bent over him, her breasts gently sliding up and down the middle of his back.

As her hands moved onto his broad shoulders, he quickly turned, and the movement made Sarah fall into his arms. Sarah looked into his eyes and said, "I love you." Gavin looked deeply into hers, and said, "You are my life, and I would give it in an instant for you."

They kissed passionately, their tongues exploring each-other's waiting mouth. Gavin's hands traced the shape of her backbone until they reached her beautifully-shaped bottom. His touch was like electricity passing through her body as she arched backwards. She threw her head back, and her breasts glistened in the candlelight, its gleam reflecting off the oils she had used. Gavin kissed her belly button, another one of Sarah's erogenous zones he had discovered. Sarah recoiled once again, this time grabbing Gavin's head, and began kissing him, biting him and licking his face. He took hold of her shimmering body and in one swift manoeuver turned her and laid her on the bed.

Sarah's expression was one of wanton lust. She wanted him right there and then, and she knew her lover was not going to disappoint her. They were both aroused – the erections of Sarah's nipples and Gavin's penis were clear to see. Gavin's hips gently persuaded Sarah's thighs apart, and her eyes widened as he entered her. Her nails dug into his back, which made his thrusts so much more powerful, and Sarah let out a little scream of delight as his penis swelled inside of her. Droplets of perspiration were standing out against the oiled skin of both of their bodies as their love embrace increased its intensity. They could hold back no longer and climaxed simultaneously, screaming and growling; they then fell back onto the bed panting and gasping for air.

After they had regained control of their emotions, Gavin noticed Sarah had removed the Clingfilm from her arm. The tattooist had done a remarkable job covering up the scar, and returning the tattoo to its former glory. He couldn't understand why she had the tattooist go around the actual knife marks in gold. Asking Sarah about this, he said, "Your tattoo looks great now...but why did you have the knife marks outlined in gold?"

"I haven't," replied Sarah.

"Take a look in the mirror," replied Gavin.

Sarah jumped out of bed, and ran across the room to the mirror. When she arrived at the looking glass she gasped. "That wasn't there when I left the tattooist this morning!" she said.

"How strange," said Gavin as he got out of bed and walked over to her.

"It's not a tattoo – it's...it's glowing," said Sarah.

"How can that be?" asked Gavin, taking a closer look.

"I shall ask Tamara what it means," said Sarah, reaching for her phone.

Sarah depressed the special button she now had on her phone, and Tamara answered. "Hi, Tamara...my knife scar has started to glow...do you know what that might mean?"

"I will be right over," said Tamara,

She instantly materializing in front of the naked couple. "Let me see it."

Sarah turned her shoulder to show Tamara the scar. Gavin put his hands over his manhood, and limped briskly into the bathroom.

"Change now!!" ordered Tamara.

Both of them were transformed into their warrior state. Out from a darkened corner walked Dewhirst. He was translucent.

"Put your weapons down, they are not needed," said the Deity.

Tamara bowed her head and said, "Mr. Dewhirst – I feared the worst!"

"Listmaker, you and your sister are to be vigilant! Keep John Smith doing his work, but have a care, things are not always as they seem. All is not well in the Other Realm – Atkinson and I do not agree on what direction to take, so have your wits about you. Bring to me the human known as Gavin Jackson," demanded Dewhirst.

"But what has…"

Sarah's words were stopped by Tamara placing her hand over her sister's mouth.

"I will get him," said Tamara. She went to the bathroom and brought out the coroner, who looked decidedly pale and worried.

"You are the being known as Gavin Jackson?" asked the Deity.

Gavin just nodded his head.

"Come forth," beckoned Dewhirst.

Gavin gingerly limped towards him.

Dewhirst bent down, and looked at the human, and said, "Your dysfunctional leg is no more."

With that, the God disappeared.

Gavin Jackson turned to the two warrior women in his bedroom but quickly realised his leg was no longer hurting, and said, "He has fixed my leg! How can this be?"

Tamara just smiled, lifted her right eyebrow and pointed to his naked groin. Gavin looked down, realized he was naked and ran back into the bathroom.

"I not sure that I'm understanding any of this…" said Sarah. Tamara took her hand, and they both changed back to their Plane of Existence selves. She looked straight into her sister's eyes and said, "When you told me about your scar I was really worried. I knew exactly what it meant – it meant that someone from another realm was close. It will be like an early-warning system for you. It is because your flesh was cut by a divine weapon.

"Why did Dewhirst fix Gavin's leg?" asked Sarah.

"He has fixed Gavin's leg because Gavin, Paul and Jeff haven't finished with Atkinson Junior and the beings from the Other Realm. They will all need to be ready and strong," explained Tamara.

"But Atkinson Junior was cut into pieces! How can he come back?" said a worried Sarah.

"Atkinson Junior's life force ends when his father says so. All he needs is his son's body parts, and, just like before, he will be back."

"So I'm still not safe?" worried Sarah.

"Well you do have a habit of killing him, dear," said Tamara with a little smile, trying to make her sister feel better. "I sense a change…the rift between Atkinson and Dewhirst is large, and I think their friendship is irretrievable. A change in the top management of our company is imminent," continued Tamara.

"What do we do now?" asked Sarah.

"Be still, little one, and look after your fiancé. In fact, all three must be looked after until I know what their positions are in Atkinson's dark game," replied Tamara as she disappeared as quickly as she had arrived.

Sarah opened the bathroom door, to find Gavin sat looking at his leg, which not only was totally healed – the scars had been removed, too.

"Hello darling – are you alright?" asked Sarah.

"Well I'm as alright as the next man who has been visited by two winged warriors and a shadowy God, who, whilst in his bedroom, totally repaired his disabled leg with no other than a few words," replied Gavin.

"I'm really sorry, I didn't mean for all that to happen," apologised Sarah.

"I know, and I'm not blaming you, but why is it important for him to come and fix my leg?" enquired Gavin.

"I suppose he is grateful for your part in what happened, a thank you, of sorts."

"Hmmm, I called to see Chief Inspector Johnson today, and the desk sergeant said he had gone off on holiday, a 'present' from Atkinson, Dewhirst & Smith! This all seems quite weird," said a slightly-bewildered coroner. "I wonder if Jeff has had anything strange happen, I might give him a ring tomorrow," he continued.

"Let's get back to what we were doing," suggested Sarah, who had now put on her nightshirt with a large hamster pattern on the front.

"Sounds good to me!" said Gavin, as the couple laid back on the bed in each-other's arms.

The next day, Jeff woke up with a start, because at the foot of his bed stood John Smith. After the shock had passed, Jeff asked, "I hope you're not here in your official capacity?"

John Smith smiled and said, "I am here as a friend, to ask if you could come to my office. – there is something we need to have a chat about."

"I'm due in at work soon," said Jeff.

"No!! Don't go into work today! Come straight to my office! Is that clear?" said John Smith, in a rather matter-of-fact voice.

"Okay, I will come in after breakfast," complied Jeff.

With that, John Smith left. Jeff got dressed and climbed downstairs, towards the familiar smell of bacon and eggs. After breakfast, he checked his e-mails, grabbed his jacket, and made his way into town to his rendezvous with the accountants. On his arrival, old Mr. Braithwaite showed him into the Reaper's office.

"Hello again, Jeff," said John Smith.

"Hi," said Tamara with a greeting smile.

"Would you like a coffee or tea?" asked John Smith.

"Coffee would be nice, I usually call in and have one with Cindy about this time. She will be wondering where I am..." said Jeff.

John Smith and Tamara looked at each other, and an awkward few seconds ensued, ending with Tamara saying, "I'll get the coffee."

The three friends had just begun their beverages when a large explosion shattered the quiet and the whole building shook.

"What was that?" shouted Jeff.

"It was a gas main exploding," replied Smith.

"How do you know that?" asked Jeff.

"I cut the cords of the people involved," replied Smith.

"Who? What people?" asked Jeff.

"The people in the makeshift buildings above the explosion," replied the Reaper.

"Soo...why am I here?" asked Jeff.

"We are pretty much through with what we needed to do...you can go enjoy the rest of your day off," said Tamara.

"Ooookayyy..." said Jeff, feeling a bit bewildered, as nothing had really taken place, and it wasn't his day off.

Sirens could be heard all over the city, and a large fire and plumes of smoke could be seen rising over the rooftops. Jeff began to run towards the smoke – his journalistic mode kicking in. The sirens were getting louder, and dust was falling all around, as Jeff turned onto the street that housed the newspaper buildings he worked for. To his horror, he discovered it was that very set of buildings that had all but disappeared. He ran up to one of the police officers to ask if there were any survivors. The police officer said, "Move along, son."

Jeff screamed at him, "My girlfriend is in there – and I work there!"

The police officer looked very grim, and said, "There have been no survivors...but there is still hope son. We are still hopeful that we might find someone alive." That hope didn't last long as a person from the fire department said to him that no one could have survived such a blast. Jeff hung his head and began to weep uncontrollably, as he knew that his beloved Cindy, Don Steele, and all the people he had known there were dead. Then he thought about his strange conversation with John Smith, and sorrow turned to rage.

Jeff Clarke ran all the way back to the building of Atkinson, Dewhirst & Smith. He was red in the face and panting for air as he arrived. He ran straight past Mr. Braithwaite, and straight into John Smith's office.

"What have you done" screamed Jeff.

"I have merely undertaken my work, as I always do," replied Smith.

"Do come in..." said Tamara.

Jeff slammed the door behind him. "You have killed them all – why!?"

"How they die has nothing to do with me. When their time is up, I cut their cords – that is where my involvement ends," replied Smith.

"How cold-blooded are you?   That's my girlfriend and colleagues being taken out in body bags! You have killed all my friends!" screamed Jeff.

"I spared the life you have, Jeff. You should have been in one of those buildings – ergo, you would have been in a poor state. Now calm down!" demanded the Reaper.

The truth of what John Smith had just said hit Jeff Clarke. "I would have been in the canteen with Cindy...we would have died together," said Jeff.

"A very poetic end that would have been, but, Cindy's time was up. All the people in those makeshift buildings had been drawn to that place and time for this very reason. You, however, weren't, and you still have work to do – so for now, go home. Your mother has learned that there were no survivors from the blast. I think she will need to see you," said Smith.

With that, Jeff hung his head, and left to make his way home. The short trip back seemed endless, and as he reached the front door of his house, he wondered why he hadn't phoned his mother...but he was there now, so that didn't matter. Once inside, he heard his mother screaming in the kitchen. He could also hear neighbours trying to calm her. When he entered the kitchen, he saw a police officer standing by the table. Jeff's mother saw him standing there and ran to him, her screams changing to ones of delight and relief. She almost crushed him with her arms; she kept kissing him and saying over and over, "You're not dead! You're not dead!"

"Cindy is, though," said Jeff, crying.

"I know, sweetheart. I'm so sorry," answered his mother. All of the screaming and the sobbing, the anger and remorse, eventually died down into quiet reflection, as a mother realised her son was not gone, and her son lamented a lost love.

Chief Inspector Paul Johnson's holiday had begun. The long drive south to Southampton was smooth and luxurious. He had discovered his travelling companion was called Dixie, and his chauffeur/valet was called Vincent. All three were about to board the cruise ship 'Aurora' – a new, beautiful, crystal-white cruise ship launched only the previous year. It was 886 feet long with a 106-foot beam. She was 76,152 tonnes of pure luxury, and was going to be Paul Johnson's home for the next three weeks!

This was the first time he had been on such a vessel – in fact, it was the first time he had been on a ship at all. Not being a swimmer, he would never have thought of such a holiday. With Dixie linking his arm, they boarded the ship. Vincent took care of the luggage and prepared the promenade suite while Paul and Dixie had a quick survey of the cruise liner. After they looked around the ship, they too came to the promenade suite, where Vincent was waiting.

"Welcome, Mr. Johnson, to your quarters."

"Please Vincent, call me Paul."

"Very well, Mr. Johnson," said Vincent, who seemed to have transformed from a chauffeur into a butler. Paul Johnson just shook his head and smiled.

Once inside, they surveyed the wondrous first-class suite. It had two floors. Dixie went upstairs to the bedroom, whilst Paul looked around the living room, complete with grand piano and private balcony. The complimentary drinks cabinet was full, and every spirit and beer it held was a favourite tipple of his. There was Glen Fiddich whiskey, Southern Comfort, Bristol Cream sherry, port, and in the cooler, Tetley's Bitter, his most favourite of all beers.

"I take it all these drinks in here are my favourites by coincidence?"

"Is there something wrong? Have I missed anything?" asked Vincent.

"No, Vincent, everything is tickety-boo," smiled the Chief Inspector.

At that point, Dixie came downstairs and said, "The bedroom is perfect, with a king-sized bed and a beautiful sea view."

"King-sized bed? Well, where are you going to be sleeping?" asked Paul Johnson.

"That, of course, will totally depend upon you, Paul," said Dixie.

"Oh! erm…I…uh, see…" said the slightly-embarrassed Chief Inspector.

"Why don't we take a walk on the promenade deck?" invited Dixie.

"Yes, that sounds like a good idea – let's do that!" said the uncomfortable Chief Inspector.

Out on deck, Paul and Dixie strolled along with all the other passengers, looking like an everyday couple, and not someone who only just a few hours back had held a gun to his head and a complete stranger. The deafening sound of the ship's horn and the tie-ropes being released from their capstans heralded the embarkation of the cruise. Dixie's arm clenched tighter onto Paul's as she was startled by the sound.

"It's okay, it's just the ship's horn. Well, my dear, we are off...no going back now," said the Chief Inspector.

All the passengers on deck were waving as the ship smoothly sailed away from its mooring. The people on the dock were waving back. It was quite an impressive sight, and the Chief was enjoying it, even though he thought he wouldn't. Two more toots of the ship's horn, and the vessel had cleared the dock, and the adventure had begun.

The passengers started to make their way back to their cabins to unpack and get ready for their voyage. Paul Johnson asked Dixie to come and sit on one of the chairs on the promenade deck.

"What do you know about me?" asked the Chief Inspector.

"All I need to know," replied Dixie.

"What does that mean?"

"I work for the company, as does Vincent. Our role is simple, we make things better."

"How large a firm is Atkinson, Dewhirst & Smith?"

"It's always as large as it needs to be," answered Dixie.

This is like questioning a suspect down at the nick – only information seemed to come easier from criminals, thought the Chief.

"It's just, I thought it was the two in the Other Realm thingie, Tamara, John Smith and the Sunny Acres Mob," said the Chief.

"They are just the visible front, with the exception of Atkinson and Dewhirst. We are many, and all have a role to play in the circle of Death and Life."

"I see...so...why is it you are here with me? What is your purpose?" asked Johnson.

"To grant you your every wish," was the simple reply.

"Ahh, a bit like a genie offering me three wishes," quipped Johnson.

"Well...not really...genies are from stories in books. I am the real thing, and I can grant endless wishes," said Dixie, striking a pose very much like Tamara, with her right eyebrow raised.

"It seems it is good to be me at this moment in time," said Johnson.

"Indeed it is," answered Dixie.

Atkinson was sitting on his throne-like chair snarling, when Dewhirst returned to his domain.

"Where have you been, Scribe?"

"You call me 'Scribe' as if it's the only thing I can do. I share in the reaping, because you seem no longer to be able to do it, Reaper."

"How dare you talk to me this way! I could..."

Dewhirst cut him off, saying, "You could what, Reaper? I have let your overwhelming ego run away with you long enough!"

"I can finish your existence right now!" snarled Atkinson.

"Go on, then, you old fool...go on! I am waiting!" teased Dewhirst.

"It does not fit in with my plans to terminate your existence yet," growled Atkinson.

"Your termination of me would end you too!" snapped Dewhirst.

"Do you think I don't know this?" enquired Atkinson.

"And your army of elementals are going to put your idiot offspring in charge?" enquired Dewhirst.

"Do you think your offspring can stop him?" asked Atkinson.

"They have twice before..." retorted Dewhirst.

"They?!" said Atkinson.

"Yes, they! I knew the last time you pulled that little stunt with the asteroid that one day you would try it again! So, I have made preparations to stop you!" said Dewhirst.

"We shall see," said Atkinson, not quite as confident as he once was. Atkinson stormed out of the cavern, and with one sweep of his right arm, he ended the existence of twelve elementals that were in his way. As he was leaving, Dewhirst taunted, "You have just demonstrated how weak your little 'army' will be when a tired Deity like you can sweep aside twelve of them in one go! Imagine what strong, young Gods could do with them! If you want to send them all to their termination, feel free! I will enjoy watching the sport!" quipped Dewhirst.

"I am ready to end all things right now!" screamed Atkinson.

Dewhirst stepped right up to his face and said, "Then do it!!"

Atkinson backed off for the first time in his existence, and the feeling wasn't good.

"Sooo, old friend, what now?" asked Dewhirst.

"I will do everything in my power to bring to and end the reign of the humans!" roared Atkinson.

"And I will do everything in my power to save them!"

At the police station, Detective Inspector Harry Scrivens was settling into his new role as Chief Inspector for the next three weeks. He was going to make sure everything was run correctly. He sat in the Chief's chair with his elbows on the desk...and it felt ohhh sooo good. He knew that one day, a desk and chair like this would be his. He began to look in the desk drawers. All but one had the kind of things a Chief Inspector would have in them. All, that is except one of them – the bottom one was locked. He phoned the front desk to ask for the key, but to his dismay, the answer was that the Chief always carried that key on his person.

Maybe he has left it at home, thought the inquisitive understudy.

"Where does the Chief Inspector live? I really need access to everything!" said the new Chief.

"I'm afraid the Chief Inspector's house was totally destroyed...he lost everything he had, but never replaced it. He has basically lived here working 24/7 for the last year," was the reply from downstairs.

D.I. Harry Scrivens sat back and looked down at the locked drawer, theorising about its contents. There was a knock on his door and Police Officer Harper walked in.

"I have taken a call from a woman on Dale Avenue. She says a large hole has appeared in her garden."

"That is surely a job for the council – it's not a police matter!" said D.I. Scrivens.

"I know that, Sir...but she says there is something strange inside it, looking out," answered the police officer.

"I'll get my jacket – let's go investigate this strange hole in the ground," said D.I. Scrivens. The locked drawer would have to wait.

An unmarked police car pulled up outside No. 66 Dale Avenue, and Detective Inspector Harry Scrivens and Police Officer Linda Harper alighted the vehicle. Fastening his jacket, D.I. Scrivens knocked on the door. A middle-aged woman with her hair tied up in a scarf came to the door.

"It's round the back, but I'm not coming! I've seen enough, thank you very much!" said the woman, closing the door.

D.I. Scrivens looked at P.O. Harper and said, "Are all the inhabitants around here like her?"

"No, Sir. Most of them are amiable and polite, I don't know what her problem is."

They both walked around to the back garden and up to the 2 x 2 foot hole in the ground and peered inside.

"She is right, Sir, I can hear what sounds like grunting!"

"Yes, I can hear it too but we can't get much closer because of the heat coming from it," he observed.

"What could you see, Sir, because I'm not sure what I saw," said Police Officer Harper.

"I'm not sure, it looked to me like some sort of black animal with glowing eyes – maybe a cat? Call the RSPCA to check it out.

Maybe Miss Cordial in there threw her cat down the hole, who knows? All I know is it is not police work! Now, let's get back," said a ruffled Detective Inspector.

As the stand-in Chief arrived back at the police station, the mood of the place had changed.

"What's going on?" asked D.I. Scrivens.

"It seems we have a gang of thugs going around town bullying shopkeepers and stealing from them," said desk sergeant Glenn Simpson.

"I take it you are dealing with it?" asked Scrivens.

"We are trying, sir, but they are quite brutal...they have already hurt several of our officers," answered the desk sergeant.

"How many of them are there?"

"About a dozen, sir," replied the sergeant.

"Well let's get it sorted quickly," said the stand-in Chief.

Easy for you to say, Chief Inspector Johnson would have been out with my lads! thought the overwhelmed sergeant.

The mob in question had been stopped by three police officers outside an old Tudor building, but the officers were receiving a beating from the thugs, when an elderly gentleman around 80 years old came out from the building and said, "Can you boys stop hurting those police officers please?"

"Or else what, you doddery old fool?" said one of the thugs as all the rest of them burst into spontaneous laughter.

"Or I will have to hurt you all," replied the bespectacled gentleman.

"You stupid old git!" blurted the thug with the biggest mouth as he dropped an unconscious police officer to the ground and walked towards him. At that point, another elderly gentleman came out of the building and asked, "Do you need assistance, Mr. Braithwaite?"

"No thank you, Mr. Jones. There are only twelve of them," said Mr. Braithwaite coolly.

The thug turned to his friends to laugh at what the 'stupid old git' had just said. To his horror, his friends lay unconscious and bleeding on the ground, and the 'silly old git' in question was standing right in front of him. Before he knew what was happening, this six-foot-four man had been lifted off the ground by his neck, and was gasping frantically for breath.

"Please...please...put me down...I...I'm s...s...sorry..." rasped the man, his colouring turning a ghastly reddish-blue.

"Are you going to be a good boy?"

"Y...Yes...please...please...don't hurt me..." pleaded this 'hard' man, as his blue jeans darkened with his urine. His gang, although dazed, bleeding and in pain, regained consciousness and witnessed their leader being reduced to tears and wetting himself at the hands of an octogenarian. At that point, Braithwaite threw him at the pile of sobbing wimps and said, "If I hear you have been breaking the law in this town again, I will have to spank your bottoms! Is that clear?"

The sound of arriving sirens and police officers running towards the incident brought an end to the fracas.

"Good day, officers. I have just come out and found these youngsters and some of your comrades...it seems they have apprehended them," said Braithwaite.

The police officers stared dubiously at their unconscious colleagues sprawled about amongst the thugs. Shrugging, they bundled all of the thugs into the police van. One of them asked Mr. Braithwaite had he witnessed the fight.

"No officer, I'm afraid I arrived just a minute before you good people did. It was all over or I might have been able to lend a hand," said the old gentleman.

"Thank you, sir, but it seems our officers had it under control. We wouldn't want you to get hurt, would we?" said the police officer with a smile. The police van pulled away, and Mr. Braithwaite strolled back into the building.

"Is everything alright, Mr. Braithwaite?" asked John Smith.

"Never better, Mr. Smith – thank you for asking," smiled the old man.

"What was all that about?" queried Tamara.

"Oh, just one of the clerks having a bit of fun.." answered Smith.

Back at the police station, the thugs had been put into cells, claiming it wasn't the police that caught them – and it was a demented, ninja-type person. The police, however, preferred the theory that their colleagues had apprehended them.

"He was called Braithwaite!" shouted one of the black-eyed and beaten thugs.

"Braithwaite?" said the unbelieving desk sergeant, his mouth hanging open. A wry smile played upon his lips.

"Why is that important?" demanded Scrivens.

"He's a grey suit-wearing accountant who works at Atkinson, Dewhirst & Smith, the local accountancy firm," said Glenn Simpson.

"Isn't that the company that sent Chief Inspector Johnson on holiday?" enquired Scrivens.

"Indeed it is, Sir, but I would…"

"Let me stop you there sergeant, I don't believe in coincidence, and I don't like names coming up twice! I will look into what they are saying," said the Detective Inspector, taking charge. He was out of the door before the sergeant could inform him that Mr. Braithwaite was over eighty years old and was not, in fact, a ninja type person.

The Detective Inspector pulled up outside the old Tudor building. He alighted, and took a long look at its façade. It looked wonderful, with the sun shining on the leaded windows, and the Jacobean oak timbers were magnificent. But he was here on official police business – not a history assignment. He walked through the main doors, to find John Smith chatting with an elderly gentleman.

"Can I help you?" queried Smith.

"I am here on official police business," said D.I. Scrivens, flashing his badge.

"Oh, I see...we had better go into my office," replied Smith.

"I need to see the person in charge," demanded Scrivens.

"Well...as Mr. Atkinson and Mr. Dewhirst are not here, that would be me. Smith's the name, John Smith. So if you would kindly come this way, we can sort this out in my office" said the Reaper.

"Oh...okay...after you," said the Detective Inspector, firmly put in his place.

Once in the office, John Smith said, "Please take a seat, Detective Inspector Scrivens...would you like some tea?"

"No thank you, I need to get on with things," was the reply.

"Fine. How can I help you?" asked Smith.

"You have an employee named Braithwaite?"

"Indeed we do," affirmed Smith.

"He has been accused of attacking some young people outside these premises earlier today."

Trying not to laugh, Smith said, "How many young people?"

"Twelve...he allegedly overcame this hoodlum bunch by using ninja-type skills," replied the Detective Inspector.

At this point Tamara let out a little giggle. The Detective was so intent on his purpose he had not noticed her sitting in the corner of Smith's office.

"I fail to see the funny side of this! I am not having a vigilante on the street during my watch!" retorted Scrivens.

"Sorry," said Tamara, trying desperately to keep her face straight.

"We will get to the bottom of this," said Smith, as he called for Mr. Braithwaite to come into his office. A few minutes later there was a gentle tapping on the door.

"Come in," said Smith. Mr. Braithwaite shuffled into the office. Scrivens asked, "Is this some kind of joke?"

"Do you know any ninja skills, Mr. Braithwaite?" asked Smith.

"I don't think so, sir...unless it has something to do with my Zimmer frame," replied the octogenarian.

"This...is Mr. Braithwaite!?" enquired the disbelieving Detective Inspector.

"Yes, this is our Mr. Braithwaite."

"Do you need to read him his rights?" said Tamara.

"Surely there is some mistake – how could this man have taken out twelve healthy young men?" gaped D.I. Scrivens.

"I think I'm a bit too old for taking young men out, sir. Sixty years ago, I could've taken them out and shown them a darned good time, but I'm not one for going out much these days – my legs aren't what they used to be I'm afraid, sonny," said Braithwaite.

Tamara smirked again, much to the Detective Inspector's displeasure.

"I'm sorry Mr. Scrivens, but I really do think you have the wrong man," said Tamara.

"It would appear so. I'm sorry to have troubled you, Mr. Braithwaite. I will take no more of your time – good day," said D.I. Scrivens as he made a quick exit from the office and building feeling very embarrassed.

On arriving back at the police station, the desk sergeant said, "I was trying to tell you sir."

"I know...I should have listened to your local knowledge. Add wasting police time to their long list of offenses."

"It's already there," said the desk sergeant, who was now warming to his new boss. He liked it when someone admitted they were wrong.

As the stand-in Chief sat down in his chair he laughed as he told Police Officer Harper of his ordeal with the accountants. "When they brought him in, I was expecting Chuck Norris...but it was Mr. Magoo! The very thought that this dusty old relic could've laid out that gang of thugs! Well, I nearly burst into spontaneous laughter!" They both laughed at the very thought of it.

D.I. Scrivens' phone rang. "It's the RSPCA wanting to talk to you," said Glenn Simpson.

"Hello... D.I. Scrivens here, how can I help you?"

"Hello, this is Jack Higgins...we have a problem. The animal you told us to investigate is no kind of animal I have ever dealt with. We couldn't even get close enough to the hole to see the beast...but I don't know of any animal that could live in that kind of heat! We manage to stand a couple of feet away, and that was only for a few seconds."

"I will send someone around for a closer inspection," said Scrivens.

He put the phone down and looked at Police Officer Harper.

"I will have to send someone round to investigate that damned hole on Dale Avenue again...the RSPCA say it's out of their hands."

"I will take P.O. Edwards and check it out for you, if you would like," said Linda Harper.

"Yes, let me know if anything has changed," instructed the Detective Inspector.

At his mother's house, Jeff was pondering upon what to do now. It was as if his whole life had come to a full stop. His mother was trying to keep him positive, but it was hard work. Jeff could not see a reason to go on. Was it fate that placed him in John Smith's office yesterday? Or had other things been put into motion? He needed to find out why he had lived, and everybody else had died. He decided to go back to Atkinson, Dewhirst & Smith.

On arriving, Mr. Braithwaite said that Mr. Smith was expecting him. This puzzled the young, out-of-work reporter, but he went along with the old gentleman.

"Hello, Jeff...do come in," said Smith.

"Hello," replied Jeff in a low voice.

"I have been expecting you, would you like a drink of anything?" asked Smith.

"I will take a Coke if you have it," said Jeff.

Tamara elegantly rose from her chair and removed an ice-cold Coke from drinks cabinet; she then poured it into a glass for Jeff. It was in fact the best Coke Jeff had ever tasted.

"You knew I would be dead if I had gone to work, so you didn't cut my cord, and you saved my life," said Jeff.

"No, Jeff...your cord wasn't there for me to cut. I had no decision to make. If your cord is in the Realm of Death, then I cut it — it is really that simple. I saved you from being horribly disfigured and leading a life of disability," answered the Reaper.

"So I wasn't destined to die with Cindy and Mr. Steele?" enquired Jeff.

"Not at this time, Jeff. Your destiny lies on a different path," replied Smith.

"And what is that path?" asked Jeff.

"A continuation of what happened last year," answered Smith.

"My destiny is to write about what happened?" enquired Jeff.

"You are a Scribe — and the position of Scribe is going to be available within this company very soon for someone such as yourself," said Smith.

"Wait a minute — of what I know of your firm, doesn't the Scribe work in another realm?" asked Jeff.

"Yes," answered Smith.

"I would have to leave everything I have," said Jeff.

"What do you have left?" asked the Reaper.

Jeff hung his head and said, "Is Dewhirst retiring?"

"You will be retiring him — with a sword," Tamara said coolly.

"What!?" exclaimed Jeff.

"It's okay, Jeff, it will be ceremonial," assured Tamara.

"What do I know of what you do? I'm just a kid!" shouted Jeff.

A loud buzzer sounded, and Jeff woke with a start. He was sweating and out of breath, his t-shirt wringing wet. He looked about to find himself in his room, and the realisation crept in that he had been dreaming. He made his way into the bathroom and had a drink of water. Coming down the stairs, he looked for his mother, but she was out. The dream had been so real it would not leave his mind. He phoned John Smith to ask if he could come and have a chat. Smith, in his usual way, said, "Of course."

Jeff made his way to Atkinson, Dewhirst & Smith, and was greeted by the Sunny Acres Ninja. Once inside the office, he sat down. When asked if he wanted a drink, he refused – he didn't want this meeting to go like the one he'd had in his dream.

"I had the strangest dream today...oh...I don't know why I am doing this...it's really going to sound silly," said Jeff, putting his head down.

"Jeff, we are all friends here. I suppose it's quite normal in your position to have nightmares," said Smith.

"Position?! What do you mean, position?" was Jeff's quick reply.

"You have suffered a great shock, it's quite normal," comforted Tamara.

"Oh, sorry – it's just when you said position, it was like I was reliving my dream," said Jeff.

"Okay, let's hear it Jeff...a trouble shared, and all that," said Smith.

Jeff went on to relay to them his dream. Upon hearing it, Tamara's eyes widened and she looked shocked for a second. John Smith noticed the quick reaction on his Listmaker's face – it was only there for a split second – but like an expert poker-player he read it, and said, "Don't worry Jeff, I think you have to be a great deal older than you for that position...but a life in accountancy can be rewarding,"

"That's okay...I'd better be off," said Jeff.

John Smith, knowing his last remark would have that effect on the boy said, "I will see you soon."

As soon as Jeff had vacated the office, John Smith's eyes pierced Tamara.

"Explain that reaction," said Smith.

"It's the Prophecy," said Tamara.

"Prophecy?" said Smith.

"I need to see Dewhirst," said Tamara.

"You need to see me...what Prophecy?" demanded the Reaper.

"When the end of Humankind is nigh, the young will replace the old as the new sun lights the sky..." said Tamara.

"That's a little vague...and, new sun?" said Smith.

"Maybe Atkinson Junior wasn't trying to put an end to the human race...maybe he was trying to dethrone his father!" said the Listmaker.

"Maybe Atkinson Junior is a raving lunatic that needs to stay where he is...in seven pieces!" replied Smith.

"Maybe the Listmaker is right..." said another voice.

Smith and Tamara both looked about them as an image of Atkinson Junior appeared in the office.

"How can this be?" said Smith.

"It's okay, John, this is a mental image...he is not here," comforted Tamara.

"What do you know of this?" enquired the image of Atkinson Junior.

"I think we are nearing the time of the Prophecy," said Tamara.

"At last!! I have waited millennia for this!" said Atkinson Junior.

"Show yourself!" demanded the Listmaker.

Atkinson Junior's image changed to a translucent Dewhirst.

"What is going on?" said Smith.

"John, not now!" said Tamara strongly.

"It's alright, Listmaker, he needs to know. Over the last few of your Earth-bound years, I have been putting things into place. The reign of Atkinson and myself is at an end. I am too tired. Atkinson is unreliable. It is time for a change. The young man that was in the office a few minutes ago will plunge his sword into my chest, then take my place as Scribe...and will wield all my powers for the time he is needed," said Dewhirst.

"But Atkinson Junior tried to bring an end to the world last year!" said Smith.

"I am still Scribe and Reaper, as is Atkinson...when you address me, you bow your head!" commanded Dewhirst.

John Smith took a more demure stance.

"It was a failed attempt to seek out his father from our domain, so he would be vulnerable – but we all know how that ended. This time he will face his father, and the fate of Humankind will rest upon whether the son can dispatch the father. This has never been done before, so none of us will know how it ends, until it happens. I was reading the son wrong, it wasn't until I read the Prophecy again that I realised what the younger Atkinson was doing; up until that point I thought him an idiot. I will continue addressing him as such when in the company of his father, but know you this – you need him," instructed Dewhirst.

"Where do we go from here?" enquired Smith with his head lowered.

"We need Atkinson Junior's body parts, before Atkinson's little army of elementals retrieve him. Atkinson knows all too well about the Prophecy. He, however, is not wanting the end of our reign as much as I do. So if he can stop it, he will. All he needs is one piece of his dismembered son, and it is all over. Only Atkinson Junior can face Atkinson and hope to survive the ordeal," instructed Dewhirst.

"Do you really think Jeff Clarke is ready to take your place?" asked Tamara.

"The young will replace the old – it is written, so shall it be," said the old Deity.

Across town at the mortuary, the atmosphere was tense as the Coroner didn't seem his usual self.

"Where's your head today, Gavin?" asked Tom Harper.

"Oh, I don't know, I had a restless night. I drove past here this morning...Sarah had to tell me to stop," said a tired-looking Coroner.

"Speaking of grim-thing... I haven't seen her in a while...what's happened to her?" asked Tom.

"She's cleaning out the store-cupboard," said Gavin.

"I wasn't aware it needed cleaning," said Tom.

"It didn't," said Gavin with a smile.

"Ahh, I see..." laughed Tom. "If you have anything you need to attend to, I have a brain that needs dissecting in the cold box. I discovered the problem wasn't related to the brain, so it's going free...would you like me to give it to Gorezilla to dissect?" laughed Tom.

"What's all this name-calling between you both? I heard her call you Uncle Fester this morning," said Gavin.

"It's her new way of trying to get a rise out of me, so I've lowered myself to her level...and...she started it," said the Lab Technician.

"Yes, Tom. I have things on my mind. I'm going to take a break – I will be about an hour," said the Coroner.

Gavin decided to go have a chat with John and Tamara about what had occurred the previous night. On his way, he seemed drawn to a different place. He turned into Dale Avenue, slowing down as he saw a police car outside No. 66. He pulled up behind it and exited the car. The police car was empty, but he saw P.O. Harper in the back garden.

He walked around the house to where the police officer stood and said, "Hello there, what's happening?"

"Thankfully, nothing to bother you, Sir," said P.O. Linda Harper.

"What is your colleague looking at?" asked Gavin.

"Come, I will show you. It's a hole that appeared sometime during the night...it looks like there is an animal caught inside."

Unlike anyone else, Gavin walked right up to the hole and peered in.

"Be careful, Sir, don't burn yourself!" warned the 2nd police officer.

"Burn myself? What are you talking about?" asked the coroner, placing his hand inside the hole. Feeling something biting his hand, he grabbed the creature and pulled it out of the hole. The creature could only be described as a hairy gargoyle. As it still had Gavin's finger locked in its jaw, Gavin gave a little squeeze. Its bones instantly crushed under the pressure of his vice-like grip, and the creature died. "I am taking this with me to check it out," said the coroner officially.

"Yes Sir!" said P.O. Harper. "How will we describe it in our notes?"

"Call it a malformed cat, due to being burned," said Gavin Jackson. With that, the coroner was gone and back in his car. He threw the limp beast onto the passenger seat, screeching away and leaving blue smoke and tire marks upon the road. It wasn't long before he was parked in the alley alongside Atkinson, Dewhirst & Smith's building.

"Do you have an appointment?" said Mr. Braithwaite.

Gavin held up the beast that wasn't from the Plane of Existence and said, "This is my appointment."

"Gavin, do come in – I've been expecting you," said the Reaper.

"Of course you have," said Gavin.

"What do you have there?" asked John Smith.

"An elemental," said Tamara. "I have two questions: One, where did you find it, and two, how did you kill it?" she continued.

"You have questions? Well so do I!" said an angry coroner.

"Let's all calm down and sort this out," said Smith.

On sitting down, Tamara said, "Answer my two questions and I will answer any question you have."

"I found it in what was supposed to be a very hot hole on Dale Avenue. I merely squeezed it gently, and it crushed in my hand," replied the coroner.

"This is interesting...so, they are going to come through the old well...and we now know who the Sentinel is," said Tamara.

"Old well? Sentinel? And exactly who is coming through?" asked Smith.

"The old well on what is now Dale Avenue is a portal to the Other Realm. It was blocked off and sealed with fire when the late 20th century gave us new technology to use. You see, we are not allowed to use any technology until its invention...it would not do for me to lose my mobile phone in 1659 for archaeologists to dig it up fifty years before it was invented, now would it?" said Tamara.

"If it was sealed with fire, how did I put my hand in without getting third-degree burns?" asked Gavin.

"Spoken like a true Pathologist," said Tamara.

"Does this have something to do with what is happening with Jeff?" asked John Smith.

"Very much so, John. This is what last night was about, Gavin...it wasn't just your leg that was healed...something inside you was awakened. This is why you were drawn to my sister...you are not of this world, Gavin," informed Tamara.

"How much more of this do I have to endure?" moaned the coroner.

"Not much more – one last battle, and everything will be back to the status quo. Almost everything is in place. All we need now is Atkinson Junior back with us," said Tamara.

"Excuse me...did I just hear you right?" croaked Gavin.

"It's complicated...but don't worry Gavin, just carry on as normal. When you are needed, you will know. If you need confirmation of this, open the door behind John, walk inside, and see the real you," said Tamara.

"Thank you, but this is the real me," said Gavin, as he arose and left.

The journey back seemed long, and his head was full of what Tamara had been saying. Arriving back at his office, he saw Sarah up to her eyes in brain parts, and she had the biggest greeting smile as she saw him walk in. She ran and jumped into his arms. He thought to himself, *As long as I always have this, I will take anything that comes*...and once again he smiled.

ATKINSON'S ARMAGEDDON

Chapter Three

A fresh sea breeze eased the brow of Chief Inspector Paul Johnson as he stood on the promenade deck with his concubine Dixie. He was thinking life can't get much better than this. The drink in his hand was pink champagne, the suit he was wearing was Armani, and the woman at his side was ravishing.

"Apart from saving me from killing myself, is there an alternative reason for my trip?" asked Johnson.
"What do you mean?" replied Dixie.
"I don't know, it's just a thought I've been having," said Johnson.
"A penny for them?" said a different voice.

The look of shock on Dixie's face was only matched by her actions, as she dropped to the ground in respect of the legendary figure from the Other Realm.
"Be gone!" demanded Tamara. Dixie scampered away.
"I was expecting you," said Johnson.
"How so?" enquired Tamara.
"I know there is bidding to be done," said the Chief Inspector.
"A favour to ask," said Tamara, smilingly, running her fingers through the Chief's hair.
"I didn't know people had to bow in your presence," said Johnson.

"Just workers and unimportant beings," said Tamara, looking straight at him.

"So, what can I do for you, Tamara?" asked Paul Johnson.

"When you moor in the mist...add a crate to my list," rhymed Tamara. "From seven destinations, collect seven parts...the crates will be kept close to my heart," she continued.

Upon saying her rhyme, she kissed him on his lips and vanished.

Dixie returned, and said, "Wow! I had heard of her legendary beauty and almost glanced at her when she chose me to do this, but this is the first time I've seen her in the flesh! I am tingling all over...just wait till I tell my friends...they just won't believe this!" "We are good friends," said Johnson.

"Wait until I tell my associates that I have mated with a friend of the Listmaker!" enthused Dixie.

"Excuse me?" exclaimed the Chief, "We haven't mated!" he continued.

"Not yet, but it's a long voyage..." said Dixie with a smile and knowing wink.

"I see....so...knowing Tamara makes me special, does it?" said Johnson, raising an eyebrow.

"You must be a great Warrior to be able to speak her human name!" blurted Dixie.

"I'm not a Warrior, I'm a police officer," said Johnson.

"No, Paul, you have just received a quest from the Listmaker...that makes you a Warrior," corrected Dixie.

"Shall we go change for dinner? We are at the Captain's Table tonight," said Johnson, changing the subject.

Back at the offices of Atkinson, Dewhirst & Smith, Tamara returned and she was sporting a satisfied smile.

"Was your trip successful?" asked Smith.

"Indeed it was. He will pick up the crates, and as soon as he has the last one we will have Atkinson back!" said a rather smug Tamara.

"But...what of Sarah and me?" enquired the Reaper.

"What do you mean?" asked a puzzled Tamara.

"He hates us both. Sarah has a habit of killing him," replied Smith.

"I understand your worries, but I now also understand what was going on – and Atkinson Junior needs you both. You must have been part of his plan all along. I don't mean killing him, that won't have been foreseen...but if you were not part of his long-term future, you both would not have survived. I should have realised what was going on when he saved those two young people from being beaten up by that gang when all this began – if he had been bent on destruction that would not have happened," assured Tamara.

"Well, Tamara – only time will tell," answered an unconvinced Reaper.

Dinnertime was approaching, and Chief Inspector Paul Johnson was dressing for the event. In reality, he was wrestling with a bowtie when a naked Dixie walked in. Johnson's eyes widened as she walked casually towards him, a different outfit in either hand, and said, "Which one of these outfits do you prefer, Paul?"

"The...the middle one," said a stuttering Chief Inspector.

"I will wear that one for you after dinner," smiled Dixie.

"In that case, I like the one on the left," said the slightly-embarrassed police officer.

The outfit in question was a full-length chiffon evening gown. Pale blue in colour, it was adorned with diamonds and pearls. The plunging neckline dove to her navel and it was totally backless – so much so, the top of the crack of her bottom would be on show. It was sleeveless, and very elegant. He couldn't wait to see her in it. She put both garments down and moved closer to him. Taking his bedraggled bowtie, standing on her tiptoes, she expertly tied it and then gently kissed him.

"I hope I'm not being too presumptuous," whispered Dixie.

"Not at all," coughed the Chief Inspector.

She turned and gracefully walked out of the bedroom, and the Chief Inspector's gaze was glued to her posterior. He hoped tonight's meal was not going to be a long, drawn-out affair. Watching his travel partner's erotic exit did not put him in the mood for boring chitchat with a crusty old sea dog.

When Dixie re-emerged into the room, she looked like an angel. A glow seemed to emanate from her beautiful persona. Her makeup, her adorable face and her body was matched only by the evocative smell of her perfume. Johnson had never encountered such raw femininity.

"How do I look, Sir?" enquired Dixie.

"Absolutely ravishing...shall we go?" answered the Chief Inspector.

"Lead on, kind Sir," said Dixie.

"What about Vincent?" asked Johnson.

"He is not needed, so I have sent him back to our domain for the night. We are quite...alone to do whatever we want," said Dixie as she linked her arm through the Chief's waiting arm, and the elegant couple made their way to the dining room and the Captain's Table.

The Captain and all the other guests were already seated as Johnson and Dixie approached the table.

"Are we late?" asked Johnson.

"Not at all, Chief Inspector," replied the Captain, offering a warm handshake.

As soon as Johnson and Dixie sat down, the Stewards began serving the food. Everyone at the Captain's Table had already chosen their meals earlier that day, so that service would be efficient. The food was magnificent, and of course, it was silver service. Starting with the Captain and working clockwise around the table, the Stewards began serving the first course. This was to be a five-course meal. They began with beetroot-cured gravadlax of salmon, chicken liver parfait with crispy toast points, and tomato tarts adorned with caramelized onions, roasted pignoli and pesto. The intermediate course was French onion soup with asiago cheese croutes, carpaccio of beef with grana padano cheese slivers and wild rocket, and goat's cheese salad with mixed baby greens and pickled walnuts. For the mains, there was herb-crusted rack of lamb with confit potatoes and steamed seasonal vegetables, fillet of beef with truffled creamed potatoes and roast asparagus hollandaise, and roast breast of chicken wrapped in prosciutto on a bed of finely-sliced bacon, cabbage and caramelized shallots. Desserts were profiteroles with dark chocolate sauce and homemade vanilla ice cream, caramelized lemon tart with cassis sorbet and chocolate truffle cake with Chantilly cream. The final course was fine cheeses and biscuits, tea or coffee accompanied by chocolates and petit fours and a glass of sherry or Bailey's for the ladies and whiskey or brandy for the gentlemen.

Dinner had definitely been a starboard-out, port-home (posh) deal, and really a bit too much for Chief Inspector Johnson. He was looking forward to supper – and supper was sitting right next to him, holding his hand. After a few anecdotes about how the ship broke down on its maiden voyage, and hair-raising sea-rescues in the Far Eastern Seas were told, the Captain stood up and bade everyone a good evening as he was needed on the bridge. Johnson thought to himself, *I'll bet he uses that excuse every single night to escape from the boring passengers.*

Just as Johnson and Dixie were the last to arrive for dinner, they were also the first to leave. The couple bid everyone a good evening and left the room.

Once back into the cabin, Dixie made for the CD player and after pushing a few buttons, Ravel's 'Bolero' wafted across the room. Of course, she knew this was one of the Chief's favourite pieces of music, but he said nothing as he was getting used to his secret life having been read by her like an open book. The Chief was trying to escape from his strangling bowtie.

I'm on holiday, so why am I wearing a goddamned bowtie!? he thought to himself. Dixie came up behind him and said, "Let me help you with that."

"It's about to get ragged off and thrown away!" said an impatient Chief Inspector.

With the smallest of tugs on the right piece of the tie, it came undone instantly in her hand.

"Can I help you with anything you need taking off?" enquired the Chief.

Dixie smiled sweetly and shrugged both her shoulders forward slightly and the dress fell to the ground.

"No, thank you," she replied, stepping out of the dress and placing it on the couch.

"What happens now, Mr. Johnson?" she continued.

Paul Johnson began to undress, but not with the sophistication that Dixie had displayed just a few moments earlier.

"Allow me to help," said Dixie.

She began to undo his shirt buttons. Once all had been released, she manoeuvred herself around him, and peeled the shirt from his body. Moving slowly back around to his front, she took hold of Johnson's belt, unhooking it from its catch.

She gently pulled it through the loops, throwing it onto the couch along with the shirt. Her delicate fingers eased open the button of his trousers and then unzipped them. The trousers fell to his feet. Dixie held both of his hands and persuaded him forward so that he stepped out of them. Looking just below his waist, she said, "Commando, I like that."

Once she had removed his socks, she escorted him to the Jacuzzi in the next room. They both entered the wonderful whirlpool and enjoyed the invigorating bubbles.

The Chief Inspector was a little embarrassed to be naked with her, because she was from another realm and of Tamara proportions. Every part of her elven body screamed beauty, whilst he himself, at best, would be described as ordinary and a little overweight. After the devastation he saw no reason for looking after his appearance, in fact, in the first three months he grew a beard. He had never in his wildest dreams imagined himself in this position.

.

Dixie rose, the spa water cascading over her breasts like a mystical waterfall. Paul Johnson gasped as she waded through the water. All of a sudden, the Jacuzzi and ship turned into a fairy cove, complete with said mystical waterfall. Brilliantly-coloured flowers and the most fragile, elegant and beautiful butterflies and dragonflies fluttered and whizzed, dancing about them. Glancing down, he was now not in a Jacuzzi, but a beautiful crystal-turquoise lake. The grass upon the banks was vibrant green and lush, looking like a thick velvet carpet. Dixie was now hovering above him, and took hold of his hands, lifting him from the water. She had large, rainbow-coloured, translucent wings.

"Close your mouth, milord," said the fairy Dixie.

Paul Johnson thought he was dreaming. She now had him cradled in both arms and was flying him back to the grassy bank, where she laid him down.

Dixie was now silhouetted by the low sun as she stood upon the edge of the lake. Her wings began to retract. Lying by his side, she kissed him. Her hand began to stroke the best erection Johnson had had in years. This was the most intense moment of his life. Dixie began to caress him. The ecstasy was so great he nearly passed out with pleasure. He seemed unable to move, so he just lay there, motionless and erect. Dixie strode over him and lowered herself onto his awaiting penis. Very slowly, she enveloped him, her bottom coming to rest on his hips.

Then she began a rhythmic motion, not just up and down, but twisting ever so slightly – first to the right, and then to the left. Johnson, still unable to move, was enjoying the greatest pleasure he had ever known. After what seemed an ecstatic eternity, Dixie rose up into the air, twisted around and returned back down onto him, with her head coming to rest upon his still-erect manhood. As her hips settled gently onto his face, his hands seemed to be released from their bond, giving him his first feel of her beautiful bottom. Her glistening vagina was poised longingly at his mouth, and his tongue explored her open beauty. It was warm and moist; her juices were like nectar to the hummingbird. His eyes rolled as he tasted what was without doubt a taste beyond anything any of his senses had ever experienced. He could feel her tongue and soft lips caressing his manhood. If ever the Chief Inspector had been close to an explosion of pleasure in his entire life, this was definitely it.

Dixie was now sucking very gently, but intensely; at the same time, his tongue familiarized itself with every part of her pleasure-zone. He was lapping as a cat would lap at fresh cream.

This seemed to make Dixie increase her efforts at pleasuring him, so much so that he could hold back no more. He ejaculated with epic proportions and Dixie just took it in her stride. She allowed herself to climax, now that her Lord was satisfied. Johnson felt a tightening and a rush of fluid, it was the nectar of the Gods, and it seemed to surge through him. It felt like an awakening, and something stirred within him.

As she once again rose from him and set herself down at his side, he sprang up and took hold of her, swinging her around and lifting her into the air, then gently bringing her down so that her lips rested on his. Once again, his tongue could not resist exploring. The couple stood naked and proud against the backdrop of fairy meadows, waterfall and woodland creatures.

"What is that?" asked Johnson.
"I'm glad you asked," replied Dixie. "It is a chest you need to retrieve for the Listmaker."
"Why do I have to get it?" he enquired.
"Only you can – it is why you are here," informed Dixie.

After the time he had just had, it seemed an easy enough task, so he walked over and picked it up. This action returned them instantly back to the Jacuzzi, and the chest straight to the offices of Atkinson, Dewhirst & Smith. Slightly startled, Johnson looked through the porthole; he noticed the ship was engulfed in fog, and he recalled Tamara's little rhyme.

At Atkinson, Dewhirst & Smith, Tamara sported a knowing smile as the holding chest appeared in the office. Walking over to the box she placed a hand on its lid. Instantly, a familiar voice came into her head...*Tamara...Tamara*, her smile widening. It was very faint, and sounded like the Atkinson she truly knew, not the last few reincarnations of him.

"What's happening?" asked John Smith.

"It was him! He sounded quite weak but it was the voice of an old friend...not the demon that he was in his last two Administrations."

"I wonder where I am going to fit into all of this if it works?" asked John Smith.

"You will be doing exactly what you are doing now! Instead of being his surrogate, you will be working with him as the Reaper, just as Dewhirst worked with him," ensured Tamara.

In the Other Realm, Dewhirst entered the Chamber of the Dead. Centralised within this great hall was Atkinson, sat at his desk that was made of stone and ornately carved with skulls. The hall was lined from side to side and top to bottom with many millennia of fallen souls, all accounted for, recorded and bound in vast leather volumes. The end wall of the hall could not be seen, as it was a long way past the converging point of perspective. Atkinson sensed Dewhirst's presence and slowly lifted his head, his hand still scratching names with a quill.

"I am busy, why do you distract me from my work?" demanded Atkinson.

"Is your Army in place, Reaper?" asked Dewhirst.

"When you need to know what my plans are, I will inform you," hissed Atkinson.

"Only the Sentinel is in place, it seems," mocked Dewhirst.

"Sentinel?" roared Atkinson.

"Yes, he has already entered the well and killed one of your little army members...they will never find the Earth-bound part of your son!" scoffed Dewhirst.

"In that case, I will cease looking. I don't need him!" screamed Atkinson. "Just watch this – witness the end – just as I made it happen before," continued the angry God, as he raised his arms above shoulder level and repeated the incantation that began a chain of events just like the one leading to the end of the last dominant species sixty-five million years earlier.

"Ahhhh – the 'Almighty Atkinson' is about to end the world as the humans know it. It's a shame you haven't been there in 300 years – you might have found out that very few of them are anything like the docile creatures you overlorded all that time ago. These creatures will fight you... and their technology will shock you," said a resolute Dewhirst.

Atkinson slammed the Great Book of Souls shut, and a cloud of dust rose from the ornate desk.

"What can the insignificant human beings do to stop my bidding, when not even you can stop me?" scoffed the disgruntled God.

The resounding sound of laughter filled the room, as Dewhirst finally realised retirement for them both was nigh. He spun and walked out, turning his back on his old friend of endless millennia, his shoulders moving up and down with his laughter.

"You dare turn your back on me?" screamed Atkinson.

Within a split second, Dewhirst had turned and was right up in Atkinson's face, hissing, "Yes...I can turn my back on you...but you have a care who you turn your back on...the end is near...but not the one you want."

Dewhirst looked at Atkinson, smiled at him sarcastically, and walked away. Atkinson stood at the side of the desk and in a low voice said, "Dewhirst, take a look in that case over there on the table. I think your plan is in tatters," said a smug Atkinson.

Dewhirst's expression was one of horror and disbelief, as everything hinged on Tamara having all the separate parts of Atkinson Junior.

"Please, do go examine the contents," scoffed Atkinson.

Dewhirst raced to the box and ragged off the lid. Atkinson was now the one that was laughing, when Dewhirst turned to him and said, "And precisely what part of your son is this?"

Atkinson stopped laughing and wore a puzzled expression. Dewhirst turned with the open box in his left hand and displayed its contents.

"What?" raged Atkinson, as he found himself looking at one of his slain elementals in the chest that once held his son's body part. Again it was Dewhirst laughing.

"It seems things aren't as straightforward for you anymore...you must be losing your touch, old friend," said Dewhirst, once again holding all the cards.

At Atkinson, Dewhirst & Smith, Tamara wondered how things were in the Other Realm, as she knew Atkinson would by now have found the dead elemental in the chest. She also knew Atkinson would not come onto the Plane of Existence, and as a precaution she removed both her own and Smith's special phones and placed them in the safe.

"So it begins," said Smith.

"Indeed it does, my friend," replied Tamara as she first turned translucent, and then disappeared.

Reappearing outside a small cottage, she knocked on the door.

"Hello, Tamara," said Gavin as he answered the door.

"May I come in?" she asked.

"Of course – come on in." replied Gavin.

Once inside, Tamara made straight for Sarah and asked for her mobile phone. Sarah, although puzzled, gave it to her without question.

"I just have to get this into a safe place for now," instructed Tamara.

"Why?" asked Sarah.

"I will explain later, my dear," answered Tamara, but as she took the phone from Sarah's hand it rang, and Tamara screamed as she disappeared. On reappearing she found herself in the Chamber of the Dead. She was stood up, but shackled to the ground by her wrists and ankles.

"Listmaker?" said a puzzled Atkinson.

"Milord, why am I bound, and naked?" asked Tamara.

"I don't want you coming here armed," replied Atkinson.

"May I enquire as to what you plan to do with the Listmaker?" said Dewhirst.

"Terminate her existence!" snarled Atkinson.

"So...you will kill her before she makes today's list?" mocked Dewhirst.

"It was her sister I called...but she will suffice."

"To what end? Is it your wish to be dispatched by Tamara's little sister just as your son was...twice," laughed Dewhirst, as he waved a hand, thus releasing Tamara from her chains.

"You go too far, Dewhirst! How dare you speak to me this way in front of a clerk!" demanded Atkinson.

Dewhirst laughed again, and with another wave of his hand he sent the naked beauty back to her office.

Upon her arrival, John Smith looked shocked to see her naked and said, "Ooookayyy...this is different. What happened to your clothes?" As he was talking he was covering her with his jacket.

"You really are gay, aren't you John?"

Smith just smiled and nodded.

"I was retrieving Sarah's phone from her, and when I had it in my hand, the damned thing rang and transported me to the Chamber of Death, of all places. I was bound, but thanks to Dewhirst I was released. We really need to find the rest of the holding chests very quickly, because they are about to fire up again, and we need Atkinson Junior before that happens."

The desk phone rang and John Smith answered. It was Sarah asking if Tamara was okay. John passed the phone to Tamara. Tamara relayed to Sarah what she had just told Smith.

"What happens now, Tamara?" asked her sister.

"Well, my little one, now it begins again. We can assume Atkinson's and Dewhirst's quarrel will escalate," said Tamara quite calmly.

"Not like last year, I hope!" gasped Sarah.

"Worse," confirmed Tamara. "Their fight ended when ours ended with Atkinson Junior. This time, it will be to the end...and that end could be the end of all things, because it won't stop until Atkinson and Dewhirst are dead. There is only one way that particular end can happen – and that is when the two destined young ones thrust their swords through the hearts of the two they are to replace simultaneously. The only trouble is, one of them is in seven pieces...and the other still believes he is a journalist," instructed Tamara.

"Jeff!?" exclaimed Sarah.

"Yes, Jeff," answered Tamara.

With that, they said their goodbyes and hung up their phones.

After turning off her phone, Sarah turned to Gavin and said, "Tamara has just told me that Jeff has got to take over for Mr. Dewhirst!"

"It is his destiny," whispered Gavin.

"What do you mean?" said a puzzled Sarah.

"What's that, dear?" replied Gavin.

"You said it's Jeff's destiny."

"I'm sorry, I was miles away...what's that about Jeff's destiny?" enquired Gavin.

"It's okay, I was just thinking out loud," said the now very confused Sarah.

Gavin walked over to the window and peered out. "I must stop them," he murmured.

"Stop who, Gavin? what's going on?!"

"When they come, the Sentinel will be ready," stated Gavin, as he fell down onto one knee and screamed in pain.

Sarah gasped as she noticed her tattoo was shining.   She instantly invoked her warrior self. Sword in hand, she witnessed a metamorphosis, as the back of Gavin's t-shirt first began to bulge, and then ripped open. With her hand gripping the handle of her weapon tightly, she moved closer. The back of his shirt ripped apart, and a huge pair of wings stood in its place, and stretched out...as if they had been folded for a long time. Gavin rose from his kneeling position. He turned and looked the giant Sarah in the eyes. Sarah noticed his eyes had changed – they were still blue – but were now piercing, the pupils elongated, not unlike a cat's eyes. Gavin was now even more handsome – his naked pectoral muscles were rock-hard, and he sported a robust six-pack...in fact, the whole of his upper body was a perfect V-shape, from his armpits to his waist. Although his jogging pants were knee-length now, they could hardly restrain the thighs that were within them. The calves of his legs were hard and rippling with power, his slippers torn, loosely hanging around his ankles. Gavin tilted his head to one side, and his chiselled expression changed as he began to smile.

"What's going on, Sarah? I feel great!" exclaimed Gavin.

"You don't look too bad, either!" giggled Sarah.

"I know exactly what to do and yet I know nothing at the same time. It's as if everything up to this point has been to get me to this point in my life! I don't know what this point is...and yet again, I do," said a bewildered Gavin.

"Just relax my love, I know this quickening...everything and nothing all happening at the same time; it will pass, and you will know what to do," assured Sarah.

At that point, although she was Warrior Sarah, Slabgirl popped into her head, and she asked Gavin to wait whilst she retrieved her other mobile. On returning, she stood at the side of her betrothed, held the phone in front of them, told Gavin to say 'cheese', and then took a selfie.

"Is that a good idea?" asked Gavin.

"It's a great idea!" shouted Slabgirl dressed as a Warrior. The unbelievable image on the phone resembled ancient Greece – not because of the surroundings, but because they looked like Greek Gods.

"What now?" said Gavin.

Both of them said simultaneously, "Tamara!"

Sarah immediately phoned John Smith's office. Tamara answered, and this time it really was Slabgirl.

"You have to come see...it's Gavin – he's changed into a...a. um...."

"Let me get a word in, Sarah...has he changed into someone who looks like Zeus?" interrupted Tamara.

"No! no! It's much better than that! He looks like one of them old Roman or Greek Gods!" said Sarah excitedly.

"I will be right over," said Tamara, thinking of how darling her little sister was.

Almost instantly, Tamara appeared. Sarah ran straight to her.

"You should've seen him! He had wings, like us!"

"Of course he did...how do you feel, Gavin?" asked a very calm Tamara.

"I feel remarkably well for someone who grew three feet in height, sprouted wings and then shrank again. I don't suppose there is any good in me saying the human body can't do that?" enquired the coroner.

Tamara just shook her head, taking both of them by their hands and pulling them towards her.

"This is all happening now for a reason, Gavin – when you were at the well at Dale Avenue, were you the only person who could put your hand anywhere near the hole? Also did the elemental you took hold of perish instantly in your hand?"

"Yes," was Gavin's reply.

"This happened because no underworld being can pass the Sentinel. You, my dear boy, are the Sentinel. What you have just experienced is what I wanted you to see at the office. As soon as anything comes close to the entrance of that well, you will be summoned there. Upon entering, you will change into what you just were, and nothing shall pass you. Evidently, Atkinson has told Dewhirst he won't use the old portal...but he will. So, my friend, you are now in place – just go with your senses, and definitely not your sciences," said Tamara.

Many thousands of miles away, technicians from NASA were scrutinizing images of a collision in the asteroid belt. The images had been taken by the Hubble telescope, and they were causing great concern. Early indications were that Thisbe, a very large asteroid, had been struck by another large space object and broken from its orbit. After many calculations and re-calculations, the shocking news was that the asteroid was on a collision course with Earth. After much number-crunching and even more calculating by NASA's finest brains, the solemn fact was that the initial estimates were accurate. Thisbe would collide with Earth.

The scientists had worked out that the asteroid giant would crash into the Earth on or around Great Britain. This news was of course kept to a need-to-know basis, as unless NASA could come up with a way of altering Thisbe's trajectory, there would be nowhere to hide. This would be Armageddon – so the information went as far as the President of the United States of America, but no further.

Back in Great Britain, Jeff was trying to work on his computer, but could not keep his concentration. Tamara and John Smith kept popping in and out of his troubled thoughts. Looking through the condensation on his bedroom window at yet another grey day, he decided he would go for a walk to try and clear his mind. After walking the short distance to town, Jeff wandered aimlessly past the shops where he and Cindy had spent time looking at wedding clothes. His head was lowered, and he was not paying attention to where he was, when he heard someone say, "Hello." He instantly snapped out of his daydream, to find himself face to face with Sarah.

"Hi, Jeff, what are you doing here?" she asked.

"I don't know, what are you doing here?" he replied.

"I work here!" giggled Sarah, and then Jeff realised he was standing outside of the hospital.

"Oh... I didn't realise I was here," said Jeff, looking bewildered.

"I'm glad you are, come on in and have a chat with Gavin. We were both so sorry to hear about poor Cindy," said Sarah.

"If it hadn't been for John Smith, I would have been dead too – a little ironic, don't you think?" said Jeff.

"I think it might have been a higher power than John Smith," answered Sarah.

"What! Again I hear this? What do you mean Sarah?" demanded Jeff.

"Come and talk to Gavin," she encouraged, taking his arm and leading him inside.

Once inside, they made their way to Gavin's office. Gavin's face lit up when he saw Jeff.

"Jeff, dear boy! I was going to call on you! How the devil are you? I was sorry to hear of Cindy's passing, You must be devastated" said the coroner.

"I'm okay. What were you going to see me about?" enquired Jeff.

"Apart from the obvious with Cindy, have you been feeling anything else lately? Anything strange?" asked Gavin.

"Are you talking about plunging swords into ancient Gods? That sort of thing?" asked Jeff sarcastically.

"Indeed I am. It turns out that you, the Chief Inspector and myself were not here by chance. We were placed here by fate...or some other power to do a job," reported the coroner.

"Yes, we were – you to find out why people die, the Chief Inspector to find out who killed them, and me to report how they died!" retorted Jeff.

"What if I told you that I was not the coroner, and that I am in fact a Sentinel," said Gavin, looking straight at Jeff, not altering his expression.

"I would say you have been spending too much time at your accountants!" was Jeff's quick reply.

"Well, Jeff, I didn't really want to do this, but as it is just the three of us here..." said Gavin, as he began to stand up. Jeff's facial expression changed at the same pace as Gavin's metamorphosis into the Sentinel.

"Now, Jeff – it seems to me you have two options, you can A – believe your eyes, and go talk to John and Tamara, or B – don't believe your eyes, stick your head in the sand, and kiss Humankind goodbye. Because without you, it all comes to an end!" instructed the Sentinel.

Jeff's face was still frozen in disbelief as he muttered, "I will go see them...just turn back into Gavin, please!"

Gavin sat back down in his chair and looked at his friend across the desk. "Everything is going to work out, Jeff. You are going to be part of the new regime. This is beyond working, and at this point we cannot even perceive what you will be doing, but be doing it you will," said Gavin, back in coroner mode.

Morning broke across the Mediterranean Sea, and Chief Inspector Johnson woke to a brilliant sunrise. As he sat up in bed there was a knock at his door. It was Vincent, with the Chief Inspector's breakfast.

"Good morning, Sir!" greeted Vincent cheerily.

"Good morning Vincent! How are you today?" asked the Chief.

"Very well, thank you. I hope you rested well Sir," said Vincent.

"Indeed I did! Where is Dixie this morning?" asked Johnson.

"Dixie is preparing your bath, Sir," answered Vincent, as he turned and left the room.

Paul Johnson lifted the silver-domed cover from its plate, and a waft of steam rose upwards, filling the room with the aroma of bacon, eggs, sausages and fried tomatoes. The Chief Inspector picked up his knife and fork, and tucked into the best breakfast he had ever tasted.

As he was polishing off the last piece of toast, Dixie entered the room.

"What happened to you?" asked Paul Johnson.

"I had your bath to prepare," she said.

"I see," said Paul.

"If you are ready, I will bathe you," invited Dixie.

"Well in that case, I am ready!" said an eager Chief Inspector.

Dixie took hold of Paul Johnson's hand, and led him to the en suite. Once there, she undressed him from his nightclothes and took off what she was wearing. Then, stepping backward into the Jacuzzi, she pulled the Chief Inspector in with her. Paul Johnson, remembering his last visit to the Jacuzzi, put up no resistance whatsoever. As soon as his toes hit the water, he noticed that through the porthole in the bathroom, the beautiful daybreak had misted over.

His heart began to race in anticipation of what was to come. Dixie pulled the Chief into the middle of the Jacuzzi, and then let herself slip under the water. When she re-emerged, she had shoulder-length straight black hair with a fringe running along her eyebrow line. The black eyeliner rimming her eyes was thick and elongated. Paul Johnson looked around in wonder, and found himself in what appeared to be an ancient Egyptian palace. He was quite bald...except for a tail of thick, black, plaited hair emanating from the left-hand side of his head. Dixie had now been joined by two slave girls, and all three of them began to bathe him. The two girls that had joined them were of a fuller figure than Dixie, with quite ample breasts. Dixie had a golden plate in her hand with all sorts of exotic fruits...some of them Paul Johnson had never seen before, but some were recognizable to him.

She began to feed him, first with a fig...and then a piece of mango, whilst the two slave girls were washing him gently. He felt every bit a King. Whilst Dixie fed him the mango, one of the slave girls was holding his penis whilst the other one lovingly washed it. This carried on – one of the women holding different parts of his anatomy whilst the other one washed it. He never flinched a muscle the whole time he was being bathed. Dixie once again led the Chief Inspector by the hands out of the bath. The two slave girls bowed as he left the water. Another four slave girls were waiting for the couple as they emerged from the luxurious bath, wrapping them in fine robes.

When they were dry, the girls proceeded to dress the King and his Queen in full regalia. Johnson's robe was made of pure silk with golden thread...it was long and almost touched the ground. His headdress was just like the one Pharaoh Tutankhamen had worn. He remembered this from childhood, once having painted a picture of the ancient King's Death Mask. Dixie was adorned with a sheer golden gown that looked like it could have been made from gossamer – it was very simple, yet extremely beautiful. Like the King's, it was full-length and flowing, and she looked every bit the Egyptian Queen. As the Royal Couple sat upon their respective thrones, a large gong sounded, and the words, "Enter with the Pharaoh's gift!" were shouted. Two men carried in a box and presented it to the King.

"A gift, oh Great King, as a token of our loyalty," said one of the men. Both had their heads bowed. The Pharaoh received the box and it instantly vanished, transporting the two of them back to the Jacuzzi. The Chief felt great – each time this happened he felt stronger and ever more positive. Dixie smiled at him and pushed herself away from the side wall of the Jacuzzi into Paul Johnson's arms.

"Is there anything else I can do for you, Sire?" she said with a giggle in her voice.

"Well, I'm already clean..." said the Chief.

"I wasn't thinking of anything clean...quite the reverse, actually," said Dixie.

They both began to laugh, and the couple submerged into the water.

Once again, a chest appeared in the office of John Smith. Tamara quickly removed its contents and placed it with the other part she already had. This time, the voice in her head was stronger. "This is taking a long time, Tamara...can it be sped up in any way?"

"It cannot, my love, it has to be done precisely, I'm afraid," answered Tamara.

"What?" said John Smith.

"It's okay John, I can hear Atkinson speaking again," informed Tamara.

"I see...how is he sounding?" said a still-unconvinced Smith.

"Trust me John, it will all work out fine," she assured.

"How are you collecting these parts without Atkinson or Dewhirst knowing?" enquired John.

"They are not expecting Chief Inspector Paul Johnson to be doing the collecting. They think it will be Gavin or Sarah, as they have the strength to go into these realms, whereas Johnson doesn't. If Atkinson takes hold of Johnson, he is dead," said Tamara.

"Is it all going to be this easy?" asked John.

"In a word – no!" said Tamara. "Atkinson will be aware of what is going on soon...and then our little plan will get harder," she continued.

"Do you think Johnson is aware of that?" asked Smith.

"Absolutely not!" was Tamara's quick response.

Back onboard the Aurora, lying in the Jacuzzi with Dixie in his arms, Chief Inspector Paul Johnson was re-affirming his belief that life is great, and was going to get even better. He hadn't noticed the storm clouds on the horizon – and that they were heading his way.

The Captain of the vessel had been alerted to the unreported storm, and was already on the bridge.

"Didn't we get any reports of this storm?" demanded the Captain.

"No, Captain, it just appeared on the radar – and is apparently heading our way," said the Officer of the Watch.

The storm was indeed heading their way, and was travelling at great speed – but the ship's crew could not see it because it was in another domain...to the crew and passengers, the day was absolutely clear and the sun was shining. The Captain ordered the officer in charge to have the meteorology equipment checked.

The offices of Atkinson, Dewhirst & Smith loomed in front of Jeff Clarke as he wandered from the coroner's office to that very place, with no real awareness of having done so. His mind was still seeing Gavin morphing into some fantastical creature and then back into himself. He knew about Sarah's ability to change form, but this was happening much too quickly, and his head was all over the place.

"Be still, my young friend. Accept what is happening and reap the reward," said a dark but somewhat comforting voice from behind him.

"What!?" screamed Jeff, turning around quickly. He then froze solid to the ground. Standing in front of him was Atkinson Junior. His head and right arm were in perfect focus, but the rest of him was blurred.

"No...no...no more ! I can't take this!" cried Jeff, sobbing.

"Jeff, listen to me. All that has happened had to happen for things to carry on. I'm not the beast you think me to be, it's my father who is the beast. I am the chosen one to take his place.

You are the chosen one to replace Dewhirst. Without you, the Prophecy cannot be fulfilled. I am weak at this time, but as Johnson makes me stronger, I will share my strength with you, and you will take your rightful place by my side," said the apparition.

Jeff simply fainted. It had all become too much for him. As he did, he fell into the arms of Tamara, who had been drawn outside to where he was standing.

Jeff woke inside John Smith's office, with Tamara holding his hand.

"Hello Jeff – you are back with us," comforted Tamara with a sweet smile.

"I think I just saw Atkinson Junior!" said a dazed and confused Jeff.

"Yes, you did, Jeff, but not the Atkinson you know. It was the Atkinson that I know. He will join forces with us and become your eternal work partner," she continued.

"So it is really all going to start up again?" asked Jeff.

"I'm afraid so," answered Tamara.

"Where's John?" was Jeff's next question.

"He will be back soon – he is in the Realm of Death at the moment," informed Tamara.

"What is going to happen?" asked Jeff.

"Now, that is a tricky question. The last time it got this serious, Atkinson Senior destroyed the living environment on the planet with a meteor. It crashed into the Earth and flash-boiled the sea, killing half of the planet's population instantly. The debris from the blast rose high into the atmosphere, blocking out the Sun. Everything that was left simply froze to death in a never-ending winter. Now here is the thing – we know he has already set this in motion to happen again. Not long ago, he instigated a chain of reactions that ended in a rather large asteroid being removed from its orbit around the Sun, and aimed it directly at Earth. This is insurance for him in case he loses the upcoming battle. If his existence is terminated, he will take this entire planet with him."

"In that case, there is no use in fighting him!" said a frightened Jeff.

"Now that's where you are wrong, my fine young friend. Atkinson has not been on the planet's surface for hundreds of years. He has no idea of how advanced his 'insignificant humans' have become! As we speak, NASA are formulating plans to change the asteroid's trajectory, and, as soon as it is within striking distance of their nuclear weaponry, they will hit that asteroid with everything they've got – and I do mean everything, right down to the last nuclear warhead on this wonderful planet. We have been looking for a way to remove this nuclear threat upon the world, and although we cannot directly get involved, we can manipulate where the devastation caused by the upcoming battle will strike and as soon as the weapons are all released, the silos will be destroyed."

"In other words, when every nuclear weapon has been fired, there will be no more nuclear bombs on the planet?" asked Jeff amazed.

"That is correct. All the scientists working on those programs all over the entire world will turn their thoughts to the regeneration of the Earth, instead of destroying it," answered Tamara.

"In that case, what do I do?" asked a rejuvenated Jeff.

"When the time comes Jeff – you will know," said Tamara, as she handed him a twelve-inch square box that had no visible opening, no apparent top, bottom or sides – it just looked like a box made of skin. On it was Jeff's name.

"Take this home with you when you go," said Tamara.

At that point, the large creaking door behind John Smith's desk opened, and out stepped the Reaper.

"Shouldn't you have a black cloak and a scythe when you come out of there?" quipped Jeff.

John Smith laughed and said, "Only when I'm going to a fancy-dress party."

All three of them laughed.

"It's good to see you laughing again, Jeff and I see you have received your box. If your box is anything like mine was, your life is going to change very soon. Has Tamara offered you some tea yet? I'm parched!" said Smith.

Tamara shrugged her shoulders and said, "I have never met anyone who can drink as much tea as you can, John!" and she left the room.

"Seriously Jeff – when things start happening with that box, just be assured everything will work out. I was scared to death...and then, of course, I became Death. You, on the other hand, have a much higher role to play. Just try and keep it together," assured the Reaper.

Tamara returned with tea and biscuits. John and Jeff tucked in.

Chapter Four

The builders had all but finished the new police station, with only a couple of days of decorating to do. Acting Chief Inspector Harry Scrivens was sat at his desk, willing the phone to ring. *This must be the most boring place I have ever been*...he thought, as Police Officer Stephen Biggs brought him his afternoon coffee. He looked at his watch and although it seemed hours since he last checked the time, a mere fifteen minutes had passed.

"Doesn't anything ever happen here, Biggs?" enquired Scrivens.

"We have just had to call the fire brigade out, Sir," answered P.O. Biggs.

"What's the problem?" asked Scrivens, thinking his day was picking up.

"Mrs. Jenkins from West Grange Road called. Her cat has gotten stuck up the tree again, Sir," replied the Police Officer.

Harry Scrivens let his head fall forward onto the desk, moaning quietly.

"Are you all right Sir? Shall I call a doctor?" enquired Biggs.

"A doctor and the fire brigade in the same day! My god, man! The front desk will think it's Armageddon!" said Scrivens without lifting his head.

P.O. Biggs just shook his head at the ignorant quip, he being one of the survivors of the devastation. Harry Scrivens heard the door close and raised his head. *Hmmm...was it something I said?*

His thoughts then turned once again to Chief Inspector Paul Johnson's locked bottom drawer. What was inside? And how could he get it without Johnson knowing? Just then, his phone rang. It was P. O. Linda Harper.

"We have just had another call from Mrs. Edwards."

"Mrs. Edwards? Who's she?" asked Scrivens.

"She is the woman from Dale Avenue, Sir," answered P.O. Harper.

"Ohhh, lovely, what does she want? Apart from a personality transplant?" he asked disdainfully.

"It's the hole in her garden Sir...it's growing and she fears something will get out and ravage her."

"Ravage her? Run away, more like! I will get my jacket; meet me downstairs," said Scrivens, placing his arm through the sleeve of his jacket.

On the way to Dale Avenue, P.O. Harper informed her superior that Chief Inspector Paul Johnson's new desk was arriving that very day.

"Why does he need a new desk?" asked Scrivens.

"It's a present for from Atkinson, Dewhirst & Smith, and today is the only day it could be delivered. Evidently, it's a beautiful antique oak desk," said P.O. Harper.

"Police officers getting gifts from the public...that could be misinterpreted."

"Oh no, Sir! It's part of the city-wide gratitude for the Chief Inspector," replied Harper.

"This is most curious," said Scrivens.

"What is, Sir?" asked Harper.

"What can a place that is sooo boring possibly want to thank the police for?" enquired the acting Chief Inspector.

"Maybe that's the very thing, Sir – Chief Inspector Paul Johnson and his predecessor Jack Thompson kept a very tight rein on things," offered the P.O.

"Oh no, it's more than that...a cruise, ornate desks...what's going on here?" mused Scrivens.

"I don't know what you mean Sir! Chief Inspector Johnson has worked flat out since the devastation without taking a break, and the city is thankful for that! He regained law and order in this town after all the looting and lawlessness took place," retorted P.O. Harper.

"Hmmm, that may be so...but here was no different to anywhere else...the devastation was worldwide," said Scrivens.

"With respect, Sir, we were at the epicentre of the devastation. Our town was left with one untouched building – it had to be totally rebuilt. And the survivors of that one building and the City Council were grateful for all the work we put in to get it back to where it is today. It really is no deeper than that," answered P.O. Harper as they turned into Dale Avenue and stopped at the house in question.

Upon leaving the vehicle, they made their way around to the back, where the hole was, and indeed it had increased in size. The acting Chief Inspector and the Police Officer could not get close to it...in fact, they stood a full twelve feet further back than the last time they were there.

"What is going on here? You don't think it's a fissure from the volcano, do you Harper?" asked Scrivens.

"Well if it is, Sir, don't you think we'd better organize an evacuation of this entire area?" asked P.O. Harper.

"I do indeed – and that is good thinking on your part – it will be duly noted," said Scrivens.

"Thank you, very much Sir!" answered the pleased police officer.

"We shall go back and organize the evacuation now," said the acting Chief.

The Aurora was now in heavy seas – the storm had grown in wind strength and was almost upon them. Chief Inspector Paul Johnson looked at Dixie's worried expression as she observed the storm through the cabin window.

"You look worried my dear," said Johnson.

"No...I'm not worried...I've fought these before," was Dixie's quick reply.

"Fought? Whatever do you mean?" asked Johnson.

"Sorry...did I say fought? I've seen – seen these storms before."

The Chief's right eyebrow rose as his expression changed and he said, "If there is something I need to know, please tell me, or I won't know how to deal with it when it happens."

Dixie turned to look at him and said, "He knows what we are doing."

"Who knows?" asked Paul Johnson.

"Atkinson," said Dixie.

"I know. I've known all along that Atkinson knew I was retrieving his body parts. I don't know why...I just did," said Johnson in a comforting voice.

"Not Atkinson Junior, his father, Atkinson Senior...you know Dewhirst's partner," informed Dixie solemnly.

"I see," said Johnson. "What is the plan, then? And I take it this storm is not a natural one?" he continued.

"No, it isn't. When we are on dry land, the elementals can only get to us via the special phones that high-ranking Immortals carry, but that won't do them any good, because they would perish at an Immortal's touch...or...they would arrive through the old portal. Out at sea there is a different kind of danger – creatures from the depths of the ocean – the likes of which Humankind has never seen, and Atkinson controls them," informed Dixie.

"Come now! Surely we are not talking about the Kraken!" said a disbelieving Chief Inspector.

"You have a problem believing in things that aren't black and white, yet you have just returned from Egypt, where you were a Pharaoh from four-thousand years ago!" said Dixie.

"Point taken," replied Johnson.

"The thing is – where do you think the stories come from? Before Humankind found true intelligence they could be scared by things like winged horses, dragons, and all the other so-called Mythological creatures. I was around in those days, and believe me, Atkinson had early Humankind right where he wanted them – living in fear. So all in all, Mythology is one of your words...it's not one of mine. "For the record, the Kraken is not a giant squid type creature. She is a beautiful but deadly mermaid, and is controlled by Mother Nature. In answer to your question, no, I didn't mean the Kraken."

"Right then! Now I have been educated, what do I do when whatever it is out there begins to attack?" asked Johnson.

"You will hide in a safe place, whilst Vincent and I see them off."

"I am not used to hiding from danger!" retorted Johnson.

"You are mortal! You cannot survive against these demons!" informed Dixie in the strongest manner.

Begrudgingly, the Chief Inspector took on board his travelling partner's advice. He was to stay in the room with Vincent, and Vincent was only to answer the door to her. As she left the cabin, she looked back at Johnson and gave him a reassuring smile. As he returned the smile, it hid the feelings he had building up inside of him for this strange but wonderfully forceful girl.

Back on dry land, Tom Harper had arrived back at work after having, for him, an unusual morning off. "Hi, Gavin, I'm back!" announced Tom.

"Hello Tom," answered Gavin.

"Helloooo Tommeee!" shouted Sarah from another room.

"What are you doing in the instrument room!?" enquired Tom.

"Cleaning!" answered Sarah.

"Ohhh, god!" exclaimed Tom, as he ran into the instrument room. On entering he stopped in his tracks, as Sarah was leaning over the table polishing it. Her very small tartan miniskirt was riding high up on her bum, showing her polka dot-patterned knickers.

"Where is your white coat, Sarah?" asked an embarrassed Tom.

"It was in my way – I can't move properly in it!" replied an impish Sarah.

Tom turned his head, murmured a few words to himself, and left the room. Two or three minutes later Sarah came out properly attired in her white coat, and said, "It's okay Tom, I'm used to having that effect on the opposite sex...in fact, Gavin is the only guy who has ever looked twice at me."

"There's nothing wrong with the way you look, Sarah. You are a beautiful young girl. It's just...uhh, well...beautiful young girls in pink polka dot knickers don't do it for me."

"That's okay, Tommy, I understand. What colour do you like?" asked Sarah.

Tom couldn't help but laugh. "You silly girl! How can I say this? it's not the colour, I rather like pink."

"Oh..." said Sarah with a puzzled look on her face.

Tom saw the confusion in his poor assistant's face and said, "Sarah, I'm gay."

Sarah looked at him and smiled sweetly. "I see! so all this time we have worked together you haven't been thinking that I'm ugly, it's just because you like boys!" said Sarah.

"Of course you're not ugly – and yes, my preferences are different to most men."

"I shall have to introduce you to my friend John Smith!" said Sarah.

"Why?" asked the now-worried Tom.

"I think he's gay," answered Sarah.

"No thanks, Sarah...that's okay, I'm too busy to have a varied personal life. Anyway, just because someone is gay doesn't mean I'll get on with him, the same applies to me as it does to you! It's not the fact that Gavin is straight that made you fall in love with him, it was because, and God knows how...but you two were compatible."

"Do you have a boyfriend, Tom?" asked Sarah.

"No. I have told you, I don't have time!" retorted Tom.

"What kind of boys do you like, Tommy?" enquired Sarah.

"Sarah!" exclaimed Tom, beginning to feel quite uncomfortable with the conversation.

Sarah opened her mouth to say something else when Gavin arrived.

"That's quite enough, Sarah...leave poor Tom alone," he said.

Tom was relieved at Gavin's timely intervention, and took the opportunity to go and get ready for work. Gavin took Sarah by the hand and said, "Fancy a spot of lunch?" Sarah smiled and nodded her head.

"The place is yours for an hour Tom, enjoy the quiet!" announced the coroner.

"Ohhh, I will!" said Tom, putting some Mozart on the CD player.

On the way out to the car, Sarah informed Gavin that she had a secret. "Go on, tell me your secret," coaxed Gavin.

"I can't, it's a secret," replied Sarah.

"Okay," said Gavin, knowing that would totally frustrate her.

"Well, if you must know..." said Sarah.

"No Sarah, if it's a secret, you'd better keep it to yourself," said Gavin.

Sarah just sat there, bursting to tell Gavin her secret. "Okay, then, if you must know...Tommy's gay!" said Sarah triumphantly.

"That's your secret?" enquired Gavin.

"Yes!" said Sarah, sporting a smug face.

"I know," said Gavin.

"Okay, Mr. Clever-Clogs, how do you know?" asked Sarah.

Gavin just smiled and said, "Tom and I do have conversations you know...and, in fact, it was he that brought the subject up so that we could set out on an even keel."

"What's one of them, then?" asked Sarah, with her arms folded.

Again, Gavin smiled and said, "I love you. It means, in this case, we started with no secrets. But as I told him, my staff's personal life, sexual orientation, colour or creed matters not at all. As long as he does his job – which, I might add, he does superbly – he is fine by me. Oh and by the way, mother phoned this morning – she wants us to go down there for the weekend to discuss the wedding plans. You don't have anything arranged for us, do you?"

"Nope! We are free all weekend!" replied Sarah with a beaming smile.

Gavin's facial expression suddenly changed, and Sarah asked him what was wrong.

"I have to be at the Gateway!" announced Gavin. His wife-to-be said, "In that case Gavin, pull over and think of the Gateway and you'll change as you arrive there."

Her beautiful man disappeared in front of her. On reappearing, he found himself inside the hole on Dale Avenue as the magnificent Sentinel. Looking about him, he saw many pairs of eyes staring in his direction through the fire and the flames. He drew his mighty sword and stood at the entrance.

"Come forth, all who will! But die you must! For I am the Sentinel of this Gateway, and not one of you shall survive this day!" was the Sentinel's war-cry.

The amassed hordes of ghoulish elementals rushed towards him, all screaming, en masse. The Sentinel stood his ground as the first wave approached him.

Detective Inspector Scrivens and P.O. Harper arrived back at the police station to the news that the hole was now making a very loud rumbling sound.

"I was expecting that!" said D.I. Scrivens. "We have to evacuate that entire area, get everyone you can out there to begin the evacuation! I'm going to get the army to help!"

The acting Chief Inspector went upstairs to his office two steps at a time, rushed to his desk, picked up the phone, and asked to be put through to the nearest army headquarters.

The desk sergeant rang him back and patched him through. Once connected, after a brief conversation about what was happening, the officer at the base told him he would get things underway. The army and the police would rendezvous at the large park on Roundhay Road. It had been agreed that the park should be a safe place to organize the evacuation from.

The acting Chief Inspector agreed and went back downstairs to see if the desk sergeant had things under control. He had already dispatched his officers to the area in question, and had police cars driving around alerting people as to what was happening.

"At least the Press haven't gotten a hold of this yet!" said Scrivens.

"What press?" replied Glenn Simpson the desk sergeant.

"Oh yeah, I'd forgotten about that!" replied Scrivens.

By the time Scrivens and his police officers arrived at the rendezvous point, the army was already there in force. Acting Chief Inspector Scrivens shook hands with his army counterpart, Major Henry Walters, D.S.O., who had pretty much figured out a plan and had already put it into action.

"Hope you don't mind, but I didn't think we had time to waste," said Walters, quite officially.

"No problem! As you say, we don't have a lot of time – this could blow at any minute!"

The police and the army began their evacuation of the area surrounding Dale Avenue, not really knowing what was going on there. The loudspeakers fitted to the police cars were informing the residents to be ready for transport. Some of them started leaving of their own accord, which on one hand blocked parts of the road, but on the other, meant there were less people to evacuate. The information about the 'imminent danger from the volcano fissure' made it really easy to get people out of their homes and onto the transport, and the whole process was completed with consummate ease. The evacuees were placed into tents erected by the army within Roundhay Park until things were put into place whereupon they would go to sport & leisure Centres until the danger had passed and the all-clear had been given.

In the Other Realm, Atkinson had given the order for his minions to push through the old portal. Dewhirst sat in his chamber, watching everything begin to unfold. He wanted an end to all of this, and the rest he believed he richly deserved, but he knew that Atkinson was powerful, and would not be unseated from his throne easily. In the quiet solitude of his chamber, he wondered if the challenge set was too great. Atkinson wielded powers beyond human imagination, and seemed to be invincible.

Was this all folly? Or was Atkinson's son really the 'chosen one', as told in the beginning of time? Dewhirst rose from his chair, vacated his chamber and visited his vast library. Upon removing the oldest book from its shelf, he placed it on the lectern. He began to skip through its ancient pages, and for the first time in his existence he looked up the full Prophecy.

The pages showed all that had happened up until that point, documenting his own fight with Atkinson, the reuniting of the two daughters, the triumphant death of Atkinson's son and John Smith taking his place. There was also a strange reference to a girl being sent back in time to help, then it read, 'These are the signs of the New Tomorrow. When all this has taken place, only then can things change, and the chosen young will replace the tired old', with the reference to the new sun burning bright.

This was not the convincing end that Dewhirst was looking for, because this could have many endings, as only he had described himself as being tired. Atkinson could go on forever…if Atkinson killed his son, and the young reporter killed Dewhirst, Atkinson would have a free hand to do as he wanted, and the one who took Dewhirst's place would spend an eternity of being Atkinson's slave. No, things didn't seem as clear-cut as he once thought. He was now left with a dilemma: Does he carry on, and hope the prophecy ends with Atkinson Junior and Jeff as Reaper and Scribe, or go along with Atkinson and try to mend the rift, hoping he changes his mind about the humans.

Deep inside a burning hole on Dale Avenue stood The Sentinel, blood dripping from his sword. Thousands of elementals lay slain all around him. His face showed no emotion, only the expression someone wears after a job well done. He picked up one of the dead creatures, and wiped the blood from his sword with it. He knew the danger had passed, so he returned to the driver's seat of his car. Only seconds had passed since he had disappeared. He smiled at a worried-looking Sarah, and said, "Chin up! Everything's ok now – I'm ready for my lunch."

Sarah smiled, reached over and kissed Gavin on the cheek. The couple then drove off to their luncheon date, and the quiet solitude of their favourite little pub.

Chapter Five

The Captain of the Aurora was called back to the bridge. On entering, he was pleased to see that the sea was perfectly calm, and all the instruments were working as normal again.

On the main deck, Dixie stood holding onto the rail, awaiting her foe. The ship was pitching and rolling in the heavy seas as she saw the first creatures climbing onboard. The rain was lashing at her face, and the howling wind was blowing the deck chairs all around her.

The Captain of the vessel was as confused as the rest of his officers as to what had happened to the instruments as the day had turned into one of the nicest days of the cruise so far. He looked on the main deck, and saw passengers in swimsuits basking in the sun.

With thunder and lightning flashing all around her, Dixie changed into her Warrior mode. Her backbone began to protrude through her skin; her wings grew stretching outward fully; she grew in stature, as her shining armour reflected the flashes of lightning. The winged helmet covered her long, red hair but it fell loosely from under its brim and down over her shoulders. She drew her broadsword and ran to meet her oncoming foes.

The Captain said, "Well, as the sea is a mill-pond, I am going to retire for a while to my cabin."

The driving wind and the waves crashing over the bows made the deck slippery, especially as the ship was pitching and rolling. The sea creatures rushed towards Dixie. Green in colour and very thin, with gills in-between their ribs, they were covered in scales, which also reflected the lightning. With webbed feet and hands, and dorsal fins on their backs, they had large mouths that were unable to open very wide. Each had only one mind-set – to kill, move on, and kill again. Before long, the whole deck was full of these creatures, and as the battle commenced, Vincent arrived, himself eight feet tall and brandishing a huge hammer. He was also wearing full war armour. This new team fought hard against the sea creatures. Although the creatures were many and seemed at one point to have the upper hand, the two seemed to be holding their own, and were now making inroads as their enemies were carved by Dixie and crushed by Vincent. Corpses were strewn across all decks as the lightning lit the entire sky. The thunder increased in volume, and yet still, more were climbing over the sides of the ship.

They seemed to be never-ending. Vincent shouted, "There are too many! We can't do this!" Dixie screamed at him to hold his ground and fight. Although Dixie and Vincent battled as hard as they could, more and more enemies were coming over the sides, when the loudest crack of thunder and strongest flash of lightning hit the decks, dispatching scores of the creatures in an instant.

When Dixie's blinded eyes returned to normal, she saw Tamara standing where the huge lightning bolt had hit. She stood there in full battle regalia, unsheathed her sword, and with one mighty sweep, sent every last one of the creatures back from whence they came. Dixie and Vincent, although magnificent by anyone's standards, were in awe of this historical Immortal after seeing her in action. The battle was now over.

Tamara raised her arms into the air and screamed, "Be gone!" As she did so, the clouds gathered into a whirlwind, then diminished as calm returned. The Warrior Goddess turned and looked at Dixie.

"Where is Johnson?" she asked.

"I locked him in his room," replied Dixie with her head bowed.

"You left him alone?" retorted Tamara.

"I was left with him," replied Vincent.

"Then why are you out here?" demanded an angry Tamara.

"I thought Dixie needed help," answered Vincent.

"You are not here to think — you should have only left if Dixie fell! You endangered Johnson's life, you fool! You will not let me down again!"

Tamara once again raised her arms, and electricity could be seen between her hands. She brought her arms down and pointed them at Vincent. A lightning bolt came crashing from her hands, and incinerated Vincent where he stood. Calmly, she turned to Dixie.

"Now, Dixie, I hope you don't let me down. the Sentinel has just laid to waste thousands of these elementals on his own. It is your job to protect Johnson! Now do so, or Vincent's fate will be yours!"

Dixie, with her head bowed, told Tamara she would not let her down.

"Take me to him — now!" ordered Tamara.

As they went inside, Tamara noticed wet, webbed footprints across the floor. She looked at Dixie, then they both ran down the corridor. Dixie ran fastest and reached the cabin first — to find it was open. To her dismay, one of the creatures had slipped by her and Vincent, and it had hold of Chief Inspector Johnson. His pained expression was plain to see as the creature grasped him by the neck. Dixie grabbed hold of the thing's head, and ripped it away from its body.

The creature's lifeless hands released the Chief Inspector, and both the creature and Johnson fell to the ground.

"Nice timing," he croaked.

"Thank you," said Dixie as she lifted him up in her arms.

Johnson suddenly realised he was being cradled by a giant woman, and Tamara was watching on in full warrior mode.

"Dixie and Vincent almost let harm come to you – I will replace them both," said Tamara.

"No!" said Johnson. "She's just saved me! I want her with me always..." he confessed.

Tamara lifted an eyebrow in her certain way and said, "A lowly worker such as Dixie cannot possibly mix with you. You are too important to us!" said Tamara.

Dixie lowered her head, and looked sad.

"So...I had better sort out some kind of promotion for when you return the Chief Inspector back to his office safely!"

This brought a smile to Dixie's face as she looked into Johnson's eyes. Tamara noticed the look of love that Dixie bestowed upon the man and said, "I see you have your own reasons for wanting him to be safe."

Dixie blushed as she took hold of Johnson's hand and said with her head bowed, "Yes, milady."

For the first time Dixie saw Tamara smile, as she said, "Do a good job, Dixie, and this domain that the Chief Inspector resides in shall be yours."

Dixie knelt down upon one knee and kissed Tamara's hand. Johnson looked at Tamara and said, "You've come a long way since you were John Smith's attorney."

Tamara laughed and said, "If you think as much of Dixie as she does you, you will bring me the rest of the boxes...as quickly as possible."

With that Tamara disappeared, and upon the horizon was the next port of call, shrouded in mist.

"We have to be careful now, Paul, as Atkinson Senior could intervene at any time whilst we are retrieving the boxes," advised Dixie.

The countdown had begun at NASA. The finest brains on the planet were working together for the first time in human history to save their world. The approaching asteroid was probably too big to destroy, so the plan had to be to alter its trajectory. After much argument, the scientists came up with the correct distance from Earth the asteroid had to be when the missiles should strike. It was a window of 36 hours from the farthest point it could be hit to the nearest point, and still have enough time to manoeuvre the giant asteroid to pass by the Earth. The further away it was, the better chance they had at moving it. It had been calculated when each different missile should lift off, so that all would converge at the same time.

They knew they only had to shift the asteroid a fraction so by the time that it reached Earth it would have passed by with thousands of miles to spare. All of the coordinates were passed to every missile silo around the world. In this unprecedented event, every missile capable of leaving the stratosphere was fed the coordinates for their Earth-saving space flight. Each different type of rocket would travel at different speeds, so those differences had been calculated, and thus the order of fire would be a staggered one, so that there would be a steady stream of blast-offs between the first and the last. The time between the first and the last would be 16 hours – the slowest blasting off first, and the latest, fastest ones last.

Would the scientists get their minute movement of the asteroid? No one really knew for sure, but it was the only path that could be taken to save the Earth from total destruction.

Jeff Clarke sat in his room like any young man of his age would, but his was not the carefree look of someone with their whole life in front of them. He wore the furrowed brow of a man with much on his mind. Opposite to where he sat was a box on the bedside cabinet. He felt so desperately alone. His life had become dark, a life of grief, solitude and the burden of the world upon his shoulders. All he could do was stare at this 12 x 12" box made of skin. His mind wandered from its dark course as he heard Cindy's sweet voice.

Hello Jeff, I am here for you, my love.

A tear fell down Jeff's cheek as he closed his eyes.

"I wish you were here, but I know this is my imagination."

I'm with you, Jeff, everything is ok – I will always be with you.

Tears were now flowing freely down Jeff's cheeks as he heard the sweet voice of his beloved Cindy.

"I want all this to stop! I want to be back at work with you...living our life!" said Jeff out loud.

Be still, my prince, for there is work for you to do.

"I know...but how will I achieve what they want me to do?" said Jeff.

The time is almost upon us my darling...if you need me, just call to me.

Then that beautiful, sweet voice was just an echo that his ears were desperately trying to cling onto. Jeff opened his eyes, and to his horror, two ghostly figures stood in front of him. After the initial shock, Jeff said, "Don't tell me you are the ghosts of Christmas Doom." One of them was a full-body apparition and clearly Dewhirst, the other was in shadow.

"The voice you just heard was that of your loved one...I have made it possible for there to be contact between the two of you.

This I have done for you alone. Now, I need a commitment from you. You must stop this moping around and get on with what you must do," instructed Dewhirst.

"Who is your friend? Is this someone else I must kill? Because you really have the wrong guy," quipped Jeff.

"Silence!" screamed Dewhirst.

Jeff sat back with a start. "Sorry!" said Jeff, with panic in his voice.

"There is much to be done, little fellow…" said the other apparition.

"Who are you?" asked Jeff.

The shadowy ghost removed his hood and revealed himself as Atkinson Junior. This was once again a shock for Jeff, as he caught his breath.

"Relax, Jeff, I am not here for revenge, I need to set things right. I must remove my father from his position. I cannot do this on my own…and only you can help me."

"You murdered two of my friends! How can I trust you?" screamed Jeff.

"Jeff, things had to be done and seen to be done for all of this to take place. Do you think I really enjoyed being stabbed in the temple, only to come back and be slain and dismembered, just to prove to my father that his thrown was safe? No Jeff, that was real pain, and I was living on a knife-edge. Had my father known what I was doing, I would have been terminated, and the world that you people know would no longer be here. I'm not asking for your trust, we have time to work that one out. I need you to work with me just as soon as I am pieced back together."

Jeff hung his head and said, firstly to Dewhirst,

"I can have Cindy with me?" Dewhirst nodded his head. And then to Atkinson Junior, "Do you really think that I can do this?" Atkinson Junior nodded his head. "In that case, when do we start?"

The two ghosts disappeared, and where they had been standing, now perched the open 12 x 12" skin box.

Jeff moved towards it and peered into its interior. He placed his hand inside and grasped the hilt of a sword. He wrapped his fingers around its ornate handle and retracted it from the box. It was a mighty sword, and was as tall as himself! He quickly laid it upon the bed, as his knees were buckling. Turning back to the box he saw it had disappeared...in its place was a suit of armour which looked as if it were for a giant, and far too big for him.

"Let's get you changed to see if it fits," said Cindy as she walked into the room.

"Cindy!" screamed Jeff. "It's true! You are here with me!"

"I will be with you forever more now, Jeff," she said.

Jeff just gazed at her in total amazement. "So...all this is true?" asked Jeff.

"Ohhh yesss...but there is much to be done, Jeff...I need you to think of Tamara..."

"Tamara? Why?" asked Jeff.

But as soon as he mentioned her name, he was transported to the offices of Atkinson, Dewhirst & Smith.

"Hello, Scribe," said Tamara, bowing her head.

"Ehhh...I don't want any of that 'Sir' stuff or 'head bowing'," answered Jeff.

"It is something you will have to get used to when you take Dewhirst's place."

Jeff suddenly realised he was wearing the armour...and was very tall...as he caught his reflection in the window. "I met Atkinson Junior," said Jeff.

"Did all go well with the meeting?" enquired Tamara.

"Yes it did," replied Jeff with a growing confidence he had never experienced before.

"Tea, old chap?" enquired John Smith.

"Why yes, please" replied the Scribe Elect.

The armour Jeff was wearing felt strange and uncomfortable.

"Think 'change'," said Tamara.

"Change?" said Jeff.

As soon as the word was said, he was back in his familiar t-shirt and jeans.

"So, you are with us, Jeff," said Tamara.

"Yes I am...and Cindy is with me too."

"We know," said John Smith.

"Why didn't you tell me before?" enquired the young reporter.

"You had to accept your fate before you could know about Cindy...or you would have accepted for the wrong reason – and then you would have faltered," replied the Reaper.

"I see," said Jeff.

The meeting came to a close. Jeff thought of home, and found himself sat back on his bed...but with a new outlook.

The hour was late in the main office of the old Tudor building. Tamara was writing her latest list, John Smith was readying himself for the Realm of Death, when the apparition of Atkinson Junior appeared in the office. Tamara smiled as her long-time lover's ghostly form was taking more of the shape of the God that she knew so well.

"Good evening, Atkinson," said John Smith.

"The newsboy is on board?" asked Atkinson.

"Yes, he was here in full armour," replied Tamara.

"What of our quest?" enquired Atkinson.

"Your father knows of it" said John Smith.

"That is very unfortunate..." said Atkinson, "but not entirely unexpected."

"They are about to dock to retrieve the third box," informed Tamara.

"Excellent, with each part retrieved I feel a little stronger," said Atkinson Junior. "I feel the time drawing near," he continued.

"Be patient, my love," smiled Tamara.

"How is it that you haven't fallen for Tamara's charms, Smith?" asked Atkinson Junior.

"Be careful how you answer that one, John," warned Tamara.

"The truth will have to be dealt with if we are indeed to work together," replied John.

"Truth?" said Atkinson Junior.

"The reason why Tamara's charms don't work on me is because I am like that poor boy you mutilated...I am gay."

Atkinson Junior looked puzzled, with an expression that clearly showed he wasn't privy to the term 'gay' used in this fashion.

"It means homosexual," said Smith proudly.

Atkinson Junior looked shocked, and he was speechless for a few moments.

"How can this be?" asked Atkinson as he looked at Tamara.

"Because, my love, in this day and age, most of us have come to terms with the word 'equality'. A lot has happened in the twenty-two years you were away. There are a quiet majority of people who accept other people for who they are. John is no different to you, my love, he just has different sexual preferences...and that is how things should be. Some of the greatest steps forward in Humanity towards anything that isn't the 'norm' have taken place in your absence...you must change your Medieval ideas if you are to run this company...and be aware, there is a common thought that the ones who are most against homosexuality are uncertain of their own," said Tamara as the corner of her lip curled ever-so-slightly upward.

Atkinson Junior looked confused, and said, "Keep me up to date with the cruise," and then he promptly disappeared.

Tamara and John looked at each other and couldn't help but laugh.

At the coroner's office, Sarah was driving poor Tom mad by saying the word, 'Why?' every time he said something. In Gavin's office, the phone rang. To his surprise it was Chief Inspector Paul Johnson.

"My dear fellow, you are supposed to be on holiday," said Gavin.

"Yes I know – I was just wondering how things are back there."

"How come you didn't ring the police station?" asked Gavin.

"Because I would get the *'Everything is running smoothly routine'*," said Johnson.

"Fair enough," said Gavin. "Well, your temporary replacement had a shaky start, but he seems to be okay now. The police have evacuated the southern part of town for fear of the volcano erupting," he continued.

"What?!" exclaimed Johnson.

"It's okay, it's not the volcano – it was Atkinson's Army trying to get through an old portal, but they were stopped," comforted the coroner.

"Is that supposed to make me feel better?" asked Johnson.

"What you are doing is far more important than what is happening here. How is it going?" replied Gavin.

"We are just docking on some small island, and it is misty…so this will be the third package. I will be glad when this is all over," reported Johnson.

At that, the two friends said their goodbyes, as Johnson watched the Aurora dock.

Gavin Jackson called Sarah into his office.

"Is there something happening, Sarah?" enquired Gavin.

"Good. You feel it too. We will be summoned soon," she replied.

Upon her very words, both Sarah and Gavin were transported to Tamara, instantly materialising in the Reaper's office at Atkinson, Dewhirst & Smith.

The Aurora docked and two passengers alighted. The other passengers seemed to be unaware of the boat's docking, they just carried on, as if still at sea. Dixie turned to Paul Johnson and asked, "I wonder what is in that wonderful head of yours this time?"

"We shall see…" answered the Chief Inspector.

Back in the old Tudor building, Tamara greeted Gavin and Sarah with a smile. John Smith and Jeff Clarke were already in attendance.

"I have gathered you all into this place so that we may discuss what we are going to be dealing with. I have never experienced Atkinson and Dewhirst in true battle mode, so I don't know what to expect – but I do know that Atkinson will hit us with all he has once he finds out…and find out, he will.

He will be fighting to save his existence, which will make him quite formidable. Dewhirst will not fight, so the only help we can hope to get from him is his non-participation. We can only defeat Atkinson when we have his son in full body."

"Here, here!" interrupted Atkinson Junior as he appeared in the room. Tamara raised an eyebrow and carried on.

"As we speak, Johnson is retrieving the third box. Then we will have a head, torso and one leg. Only when all seven pieces are in place do we have his help. I want Sarah to listen out for Johnson or Dixie needing help. Atkinson has started using elementals, so Gavin – as soon as you get a strange feeling, act upon it right away, only you and I have the power to stop them en masse."

At this point Atkinson Junior's apparition spoke. "Once I am reformed, the final battle will begin, because when my last piece- my heart – is put in place, my father will know I live. He has seen how the end may take shape, so he has already put other things into place."

"Other things in place?" repeated the Sentinel.

"Yes, Gavin. As we speak, there is a very large asteroid heading for Earth…but the scientists at NASA are working on it. My father doesn't even know NASA exists, so for now, we can leave that to them. Oh – one other thing, Sarah, when the final battle does come, will you please refrain from killing me?"

This brought a much-needed spark of light-heartedness to the conversation. Tamara then continued.

"When, and if, we get to the point where Atkinson Junior is fighting his father…that is when you join in the fight, Jeff."

At this point, Atkinson Junior again spoke. "I will not call for you Jeff, until I need you in place. I can't risk you getting hurt, you are the lynchpin in all of this. You have to understand how important you are to all of us here…we have waited a long time for your arrival. Believe me, if you had arrived two-hundred years ago, the world would not be in the state it is in now. But together, we can all turn this around."

"And where do I fit into this plan?" asked John Smith.

"Reaping will still have to take place whilst Atkinson plots his next move on us. Dewhirst will be the Scribe. We still have to maintain our prime directive, John," said Tamara.

"No matter what happens John, you must not join me in that realm...there will already be my father, Dewhirst, Jeff and myself within that place, which will make it unstable enough. If you join us, the effect could be catastrophic for us all. I am sure you remember what happened the last time we met on the same plane."

"I remember it well," recalled John.

As the mist began to clear, Paul Johnson and Dixie found themselves riding into Dodge City. Johnson was dressed in black, with two guns holstered on his hips. He wore a long duster coat and a black Stetson hat, and had three days' worth of stubble on his chiselled chin. Dixie was also dressed in black, but her clothes were figure-hugging, showing off her curves. Main Street was quiet and empty, as they tied their horses outside the saloon. On entering, all heads turned their way.

"What'll be, stranger?" said a scruffy man behind the bar.

"Whiskey," replied Johnson, trying to emulate Clint Eastwood.

"What about the little girly?" he queried.

In that instant, the cigarette he was smoking had been shot out of his mouth.

"No one calls me girly!" huffed Dixie, with smoke trailing from the barrel of her gun. The bartender's shaking hands poured two whiskies into the unwashed glasses. Everyone commenced to do what they were doing before she turned their heads.

Johnson and Dixie drew up a couple of chairs and sat down. The Sheriff, his star gleaming on his dusty chest, walked over to their table and said, "Normally, I would be saying I don't want any trouble...but I already have it. I know who you are," he said, looking at Johnson. "Hell, I've had your picture on my wall ever since I've been the Sheriff in this town!"

Under the table, Johnson's hand slowly embraced the handle of his gun, and his Colt revolver clicked. The Sheriff gulped but continued. "We are all here because the Murphy Gang has got us pinned down. They have guns on the roof...in the streets...everywhere. They have packed five crates of gold from the bank and are about to leave town with them. If you can stop them, you can ride out of town with one of them crates, no questions asked and no posse following."

Johnson's grip on his sidearm eased as he looked at Dixie. Dixie smiled and said, "I reckon we can rid you of this vermin!" as she spit some chewing tobacco into a nearby spittoon. Johnson placed both of his guns on the table, and drew a handful of bullets from his belt.

"You ride with empty guns?" exclaimed the incredulous Sheriff.

"I keep a bullet in each gun...I only need the one shot. I find it keeps me...alert," grinned the man with the fastest gun ever to be un-holstered in the West.

"How many are on the roofs?" enquired Dixie.

"There are eight," answered the Sheriff.

"How many on the ground?" asked Johnson.

"There are six," answered the Sheriff.

"And how many robbing the bank?" queried Dixie.

"There are eight in the bank as we speak," said the Sheriff.

"Is that all of them?" asked Johnson.

"It's the entire gang," replied the Sheriff.

"Well, by my reckoning, that is twenty-two in all – that gives us a spare bullet each," said Johnson as he filled the last empty chamber of his second gun.

"I will see to the ones on the ground," said Dixie.

"I'll take the ones on the roofs," said Johnson.

"Do you want anything other than drink? Something to eat, perhaps?" asked the bartender.

"Save it for when we come back inside," said Dixie.

Johnson and Dixie stepped out of the saloon as if they were leaving. As they walked into the street, a voice rang out from the rooftop.

"Drop your guns and get back into the saloon!"

Johnson lifted the brim of his Stetson by slightly craning his neck back and looked up at the man giving the orders.

"Have you seen all of yours?" he asked Dixie.

"Yep," she replied.

"Okay," said Johnson.

Upon the word 'okay', fourteen shots rang out in an instant, followed by a short silence – and the sound of fourteen dead bodies hitting the ground. The hand movements from Johnson and Dixie were like lightning, as they both swivelled their guns in flamboyant circles before re-holstering them. As the last man fell from the roof, the rest of the gang ran from inside the bank. They saw their dead comrades on the ground and only two people standing in the street.

"Kill them!" shouted James Murphy, the gang leader.

But no sooner had the words left his mouth when a bullet between his eyes silenced him forever. Instantaneously, the last of his gang was as dead as he, and the full Murphy Clan who had for years ruled the town with fear, were history.

Johnson looked at Dixie and gave her a wink. "I enjoyed that," he quipped.

Dixie smiled back, and shaking her head, she said, "Only one word – boys!"

Johnson looked at the tall man wearing a top hat and a tape measure around his neck and said, "I make that twenty-two bodies...a good day for you, undertaker!"

The undertaker looked solemn and yet very, very happy.

The rest of the townsfolk ran out from the saloon, along with the Sheriff. They were all cheering, and circled the couple. The wily old Sheriff then said, "I am now faced with a dilemma."

"What's that, Sheriff?" said Johnson.

"Well...the Murphy Gang are dead...so why do I need to give two outlaws one of these boxes?" said the Sheriff.

"Make that twenty-three boxes!" shouted Dixie to the undertaker.

"I have still got a bullet in my gun...and before you can even think of an answer, you will be boots-up. So...why don't I give you an extra second to re-think your plan?" said Johnson.

The Sheriff looked shocked – especially as both Johnson's and Dixie's guns were now pointed at his head – both with one bullet in the chamber.

"What'll it be, Sheriff?" said Johnson, as his right fourth finger caressed the trigger.

The Sheriff, in total disbelief that they had not wasted one shot, put his hands up, and the box was given to Johnson in total silence. As soon as Johnson's hands gripped the box, it disappeared, along with Dodge City and its inhabitants. The mist cleared, and the gangplank of the Aurora was in front of them. they stepped back onboard and soon were back at sea.

In the main office of Atkinson, Dewhirst & Smith, the chest arrived, and was quickly dealt with by Tamara.

"As you can all see, the quest goes well," she said.

Atkinson Junior's apparition smiled.

"What will happen when the last box arrives?" asked the coroner.

"We will be prepared to face Atkinson," said Tamara, looking at the strengthening Atkinson Junior. The more he materialised, the less harsh he looked, and the more he looked like the Atkinson Junior of old...the bigger Tamara's smile grew.

After a long discussion about the things to come, the first meeting proper of six of the eight Warriors came to an end. The other two members of this elite group were arm-in-arm, sailing back to sea midway through their cruise.

Chapter Six

Ken Jones, one of the NASA scientists, was working very late on a question that was puzzling him. It wasn't about if the missiles would do their job, or when to blast them off. These two questions had been answered, and worked on constantly over the last two weeks.

His mind had turned to why all of a sudden this huge asteroid could be knocked out of its orbit around the Sun and be put on an exact trajectory for Earth. More to the point, he was trying to calculate the size of the object, or comet that had struck it, and why NASA knew nothing about it until after it collided with the asteroid. Also, he was thinking of his religious views. He was a Christian as well as a scientist, and he knew the Bible. A part of that book was speaking to him – now and that part was Revelations.

There were parts of his holy book that the scientist in him had come to terms with as not true. However, other parts of this book he believed in. It seemed to him that the more science removed God from the equation, the angrier God himself became...this was a strange thing for a scientist to feel.

Ken Jones had battled with the two sides of his life for all of his life. Something inside told him that science would not win this day, and pondered as to what to do next. *Maybe this was the 'will of God'...maybe this was the 'Armageddon'. If Humankind wins this fight, does that mean God doesn't exist? If they lose, it doesn't matter anyway.*

A feeling came over him that he had to do something. He could not sit back and let his religious beliefs be destroyed by his scientific teachings. He put his papers in his briefcase, tidied his desk, and with his top-security status – he typed his passwords into the computer and opened the missile-firing codes. He then began altering the distance settings, feeding them through each of the separate missile launch codes.

Once he had altered the codes, he changed the passwords to random 300 digit passwords that he wasn't writing down, and then exited the program. He knew this would only be discovered if anyone needed to check the launch codes...and he also knew that there was no need to check them, now that the scientists had set them. He did, however, know that as they blasted off early, it wouldn't be long before they realised the system had been sabotaged. By then it would be too late...all of the missiles would be on their way, and set to converge a full day earlier than planned.

Ken Jones rose up from his desk, left the office and then vacated the building. He didn't go straight home, he went to church and prayed. After about thirty minutes, a priest came up to him to ask if he was okay.

"Do you believe in the end of all things...Armageddon?" asked Ken Jones.

"I believe it was put in the Bible as a warning of what might happen...not necessarily what will happen," replied the priest.

"If it was God's will, but Humankind had the power to stop it...what then?" asked the troubled scientist.

"If it was God's will, but he had given Humankind the ability to stop it, and they did – it is still God's will, my son," said the priest.

"Is that what you really believe?" asked Ken Jones.

"It is," replied the priest.

"Then I am damned," replied Jones.

"You go have some sleep – you look tired. You will find things will look brighter in the morning," comforted the priest.

Ken Jones rose from the uncomfortable pew with his head down, and left Saint Mary's Church feeling totally confused. In trying to save his religious beliefs he had doomed the planet! The full weight of his actions was now resting heavily on his shoulders, as he turned the key to the front door of his house. Throwing his jacket over the chair arm, he sat down and put his head in his hands and began to weep. He wished he hadn't made it impossible to get back into the launch programme...or at the very least, had taken advice from a priest before he took his extreme actions. He looked at a bottle of whiskey, and the box of extra-strong pain-killing tablets he had on the table. He unscrewed the top of the new whiskey bottle and took a handful of the tablets, washing them down with a large gulp of whiskey. He repeated the process ten times. He lay back in his chair and waited for damnation.

Chapter Seven

 day had passed, and all appeared quiet. No trouble from the old portal, and the Aurora was not in sight of land. Tamara and John had settled down to business as usual – List making, and Reaping, respectively. Jeff Clarke was again in his bedroom, contemplating his future. The countdown at NASA was seemingly going smoothly. Acting Chief Inspector Scrivens and his army counterparts had now placed all the evacuees into safer temporary accommodation and the sun was shining.

In fact, all in all, it was a lovely day, except for a certain mortuary technician who had spent the previous twenty minutes looking for 'Slabgirl'. He had tried all of the vacant fridges, checked all the empty rooms...and still, no Sarah. Then he noticed the cadaver under the cover on the waiting trolley was breathing.

He grabbed the sheet and pulled it away in dramatic fashion, revealing Sarah in a death pose. Her eyes were open, but all Tom could see were the whites. Her tongue was hanging out of the corner of her mouth. She was holding a little sign on her chest which read, 'Please put flowers on my grave, Tommy'.

"Put flowers on your grave? I will dance on it!" said Tom.

Sarah began giggling. She sat up on kissed him on the cheek. "Your turn to hide now, Tommy!" she said eagerly.

"Hide indeed – We have work to do!" said Tom Harper quite officially.

"You are no fun at all! You're just like Gavin when we are in here!" she said.

"How do you mean?" enquired Tom.

"All official and solemn," replied Sarah.

"Why thank you! That's the kindest thing you have said all week!"

"I'm bored Tommy...why isn't there anything to cut up?"

"Because, Sarah, that is work for the coroner and myself. Your job is to clean up afterwards, and make the tea. Three months at college has not elevated your situation...three years might," instructed Tom.

"I can't make any tea," said Sarah, sticking her tongue out at Tom.

"Do, pray tell, why?" he asked.

"No sugar," said Sarah.

"How wonderful...there really is a God," said Tom Harper as he took a £5 note out of his wallet. Upon giving it to Sarah, he said, "Don't go to the nearby shop, I don't like their sugar...go to the supermarket."

Sarah, who was sitting with her tartan-patterned tights-covered legs swinging over the side of the gurney, said, "But that will take me ages!"

"I know, so off you trot...you gruesome minx," replied Tom.

Sarah jumped off the gurney and her heavy boots made a loud bang on the floor.

"And that's another thing! Don't you have any girl's shoes?" asked Tom.

"These are girls shoe's! They're a size 3!" retorted Sarah as she turned her back on him, walked out and slammed the door.

Gavin, as usual, had been watching the proceedings from the security of his office window. He came out laughing.

"I think you actually won that time, Tom," he said giggling.

"Do you know...I think I did!" laughed Tom.

"Do you think it will dawn on her that sugar is the same wherever you get it from?" asked the coroner.

"Actually, I hope so...I could really use a cup of tea right now," said Tom.

"By the way, old boy, I'm taking said 'gruesome minx' down to my parent's tomorrow for a couple of days...would you like me to get some help for you while I'm gone?" asked Gavin.

"Only if I can't get in touch with you," said Tom.

"Oh no – I'll be on call – you can phone me anytime," answered Gavin.

"In that case, I will be fine on my own. The porters are in the office next door, so all's well with me," answered Tom.

Silence had reigned in Tom's Pathology Paradise for exactly seven and a half minutes when the door burst open and in marched Sarah, with rage in her eyes and a bag of sugar under her arm.

"You think I'm an idiot!" shouted Sarah.

"How far had you travelled before you realised?" asked a very calm Tom.

"Not very far," replied Sarah.

Tom laughed. "So you did start going to the supermarket, then?"

"I'm going to get you for that, Tom Harper!" said Sarah, standing in the classic 'angry girl' style with her hands on her cocked hips.

"Actually, you're right, Sarah...I was wrong to do that. I'll tell you what I'll do. I'm going to let you get me back. I will give you two whole days...starting tomorrow," said Tom.

"Oh no... I'm not falling for that 'tomorrow' lark...do you mean tomorrow as in Saturday and Sunday?" she said, her stance only changing by the raising of an eyebrow.

"Yes. Saturday and Sunday, you can do whatever you like to me. How does that sound?" he said.

Sarah outstretched her hand and said, "Shake on it, then!"

Tom shook her hand and said, "It's a deal. But it ends Sunday night."

"Agreed," said Sarah.

Sarah made the tea. She gave Tom his, and then took hers and Gavin's into the office. A minute later, Sarah burst out of the office screaming.

"You have cheated! I hate you Tom Harper!"

Tom just drank his tea, laughing to himself, and dreaming of the quiet weekend ahead.

The next day saw Gavin and Sarah packing the car for their weekend in the country. Gavin was wearing his tweed jacket with leather patches on the elbows, a pair of comfortable trousers for driving in, and a tweed flat cap. Sarah wore a pair of leopard-skin pants, a ripped Sex Pistols 'Never Mind the Bollocks' t-shirt, a pair of pink Doc Martin boots, and a straw floppy hat that looked slightly Australian – but instead of corks dangling from the strings on the rim of the hat this one had skulls. The couple looked as they always did – poles apart.

As they sat in the car, Gavin looked at Sarah and said, "When I sent you out to get clothes for the country, you didn't really understand what I meant, did you?"

To which Sarah replied, "Yes I did! I bought a new hat! Don't you just love it, Gavin?" she beamed.

"Yes my dear...it's marvellous," answered Gavin.

They pulled out of the driveway of their little cottage, and made for Gavin's parents' house in the country. The trip was quite an assault on Gavin's ears, as Sarah introduced him to Nine Inch Nails, Korn and Megadeth. He was more used to Bach, Mozart and Beethoven.

It wasn't long before they were turning off the road and through the gates of Gavin's parents' country house. As the car came to a halt outside the front door, Gavin noticed another car parked in the driveway. In his eyes, it was a thing of beauty – a Jaguar XK 120 Roadster in British Racing Green.

Upon stepping out of his car, he had a closer inspection of the vehicle, then quickly remembering his manners, he went back to the car to help Sarah out...but Jarvis had beaten him to it. On seeing his parents' butler, Gavin smiled and shook his hand, giving him the usual, "How are you doing, Jarvis?" to which Jarvis replied, "I am splendid Sir! It is very good to see you again!" Turning to Sarah, Jarvis added, "Always good to see you, little Miss," to which Sarah beamed a lovely smile and a little giggle.

"Gavin old boy! What do you think of her?" Came a resonant voice from the doorway – Gavin's father smiled and walked out to meet them.

"She's a beauty...where did you find her?" answered Gavin, shaking his father's hand.

"Oh... a friend of mine....who had a friend...you know how it goes," beamed his father Donald.

Sarah stepped onto her tippy-toes and whispered into Jarvis' ear, "Who are they talking about?

Jarvis' stiff upper lip began its now-customary quiver whenever Sarah spoke to him. "It would appear they are referring to the vehicle, Madam," he informed.

"Oh!" said Sarah, looking quite puzzled.

By this time, Gavin's mother had arrived on the scene.

"Oh stop it, you two children! Let's have this lovely young lady inside the house so we can plan the wedding!" instructed Gavin's mother.

Sarah ran up to her and threw her arms around her, planting a big kiss upon her cheek. "Thanks, Mum!" Sarah beamed the largest smile at her new family and ran into the house, Gavin's mother following, shaking her head and smiling to herself.

Once inside, it wasn't long before Jarvis reappeared with some tea. The conversation had not arrived at the wedding as yet – Donald and Gavin Jackson were still engrossed with the car.

"Well, father, what will you do with the Aston Martin now you have this?"

"Oh no! You misunderstand, son, this is to be your and Sarah's wedding present from me."

Gavin's jaw dropped so much, it felt like it was hitting his knees. Trying to put a sentence together, he said, "Our wedding present from you both?" To which his mother sternly said, "Certainly not! That ridiculous boy's toy parked outside has nothing to do with me! My present to you is far more useful than a silly car!"

Sarah was perched upon the edge of the elegant Chesterfield sofa, looking rather excited. Pointing out of the window with her finger to the car she said, "That little car...is ours?"

"Yes, my dear," said her mother-to-be. "But don't worry, the present I've gotten you, you will enjoy much more."

Sarah began bouncing up and down on her bum excitedly, and chanted, "What have you got? What have you got? What have you got?"

"Now, now, Sarah – we ladies must not get so excitable – and don't slurp your tea dear."

Donald and Gavin began to laugh, and the slightest of titters escaped the stiff-lipped butler.

"Jarvis?"

That one word from his mistress was enough to put an end to his amusement.

"Do excuse me madam – I've a troublesome throat today." The red-faced butler then quickly slid out of the room.

"Well then, old girl! Before you start to change Sarah into one of your tight-lipped, bridge-playing, socialite friends, do put the poor girl out of her misery!" said Donald Jackson as he purposefully slurped his tea.

"Donald!"

"Excuse me dear...having trouble with my stiff upper lip today!"

"Well...if I may...come and sit down Gavin."

Gavin came and sat down beside Sarah. Sarah inched towards Gavin and asked, "What's the matter with your daddy's lip?"

Unfortunately for Gavin, he had just taken a mouthful of tea, which inadvertently ended up all over his front.

"Gavin! Really!"

"Sorry, mother – it's just..."

"I know, I heard – there is nothing wrong with the old fool's lip, he was being facetious!"

The blank look on Sarah's face spoke volumes.

"It means that, again, I have been a naughty boy, Sarah," said Donald Jackson.

"Oh!" said Sarah...who then looked straight back at Gavin's mother with an expression of somebody who didn't really know what was going on, but was going along with it.

"Right then, you two...have you ever heard of 'The Cube?'" asked Gavin's mother.

"You mean that new building?" asked Gavin.

"I know that place!" piped up Sarah, "It's near the Phono!" she said.

"Well...your days of commuting to work are now over," said Harriette Jackson. "I have purchased you the penthouse as a wedding present.

Sarah and Gavin stared agog, not knowing what to say. A Jaguar – and now, one of the most prestigious residences in the city.

"I don't know what to say, mother."

"Say nothing! Just repay me with grandchildren!" she said with a smile.

Sarah ran into her arms nearly knocking her over. Harriette was beginning to grow fond of this strange, funny little girl, with rebellious-looking clothing and gaudy makeup. For underneath it all lay a heart of gold.

"Who will you procure to do the restoration work on the Jag, father?"

"I know a chap in the city near where you work – he did a rather splendid rebuild of Jefferson's 1960 mini Cooper. He owns a small garage in a place called, 'Crossgates'...ex-policeman, absolutely marvellous chap. It will be delivered to him on Monday, and he assures me it will be ready long before the wedding."

"Speaking of the wedding..." said the lady of the house, "Everything is now set. The church is booked, reception and honeymoon taken care of. The invitations have been dealt with a while ago, and most have R.S.V.P.'d. So...three weeks from today you will both be married!" smiled Harriette Jackson.

Sarah squeezed Gavin's arm and said, "I know! I can't believe it!"

Gavin held onto her arm and smiled back at his wife-to-be.

"After the terrible things that happened a year ago, it is good that we are all still here to be planning a wedding – many people were not as fortunate as we," said Donald Jackson.

"I'll second that father!" answered Gavin.

The Aurora was in mid-ocean, and was fast-approaching a strange mist. Dixie moved away from the cabin window and said, "Are you ready, Paul? We are about to land again."

"Land? I don't see any land..."

"Nevertheless, land we will," she replied mysteriously.

Johnson began to put his jacket on and Dixie stayed his hand. "You won't need that," she said.

Again, Johnson looked puzzled. Dixie took his hand, lead him out onto the deck, and said, "Come with me now...and don't be afraid. I want you to just breathe normally. You will see that as long as you are holding my hand when you are diving, you will be fine."

There was a look of trepidation on Paul Johnson's face as they walked to the starboard safety rail on the main deck.

Dixie gave him her brightest smile, and whilst still holding his hand, jumped over the side, taking the Chief Inspector with her.

Upon hitting the water, Dixie morphed into a beautiful mermaid with a long tail that could only be described as iridescent – as what seemed like thousands of shimmering, metallic hues burst into life, dancing in the light with each swish of her tail. She was naked, and her long, flowing hair was slowly swaying from side to side in a hypnotic rhythm with the changing directions of the water.

Johnson was stunned by this Goddess of the Sea, but was beginning to look worried as he was now very short of breath. With a minimum of effort, Dixie moved close and looked deep into his eyes. In his mind, he heard her say, *Breathe my love, Breathe.* Her beauty made him forget where he was, and he took a sharp intake of breath. Then the realization hit him that he was underwater...but he was breathing. *How can this be?* he thought to himself. *It's because, you are now like me,* answered Dixie's voice in his head. *You know what I'm thinking?* asked Johnson.

It's how we communicate down here, she answered. It was at this point Paul Johnson realised his legs didn't feel quite normal. Looking down, he saw his legs were no more, and in their place was a tail that matched the one adorning his beautiful Dixie. Dixie took hold of his cheeks and kissed him. Her arms then wrapped around his torso and their tails intertwined. They twisted and turned in the water and the kiss seemed to last forever. When it ended, she held both of Paul's hands, and through thought transference said, *This is going to be the most dangerous one yet. Atkinson's elementals control the sea through him and will already have been alerted to our presence. We must act fast, follow me.*

With that, she swam downwards towards the ocean floor and Johnson followed on behind.

They were both now at a depth no human had ever dove to before and all daylight was gone, but somehow, he could still see...there was some kind of light emanating from the ocean floor. Deeper and deeper they dove, passing all kinds of creatures...the likes of which Johnson had never seen. Eel-like creatures that had lights twinkling in their tails...pale-blue, humanoid, ghostly figures were all around, but were unaware of their presence. Shells of enormous size adorned the sea bed. Crab-like creatures with pincers the length of a man were guarding the gates of what looked like a great underwater city. Johnson knew the other places he had visited on this strange voyage had come from his own imagination – but he knew nothing of this.

That's because this is real, and not a figment of your imagination or a half-forgotten dream, instructed Dixie.

Is this Atlantis? inquired Paul Johnson.

No, my love...Atlantis is just a set of ruins caused by an angry God. This is the home of the original inhabitants of this planet. They arrived here about 20 million years before the first dinosaurs walked on land.

Arrived here? You mean they are aliens? interrupted the Chief Inspector.

Why does that sound so strange to you, Paul? asked Dixie.

It just doesn't fit in with any theories we have of evolution, said the sceptical Chief.

Oh yes, a God making a man first, and then a woman from one of his 'lesser' bones. Or do you mean the other evolution theory, which allows primates and their evolved humans to 'live together' – but not a sabre-toothed tiger and its evolved tiger, or its woolly mammoth and elephant. Humans are very easy to mould...you must be different Paul, and start using all of your brain.

Soon they were inside the city walls. All of the buildings were of round or oval construction. The police officer deduced this was to stop erosion.

These buildings are made of a substance that doesn't erode – they are just of a certain style. The home planet has three distinct styles of building. This type is for dense gravity, or very heavy pressure. There are pyramid-type buildings for hot, sandy areas, and buildings cut from stone...but very few of these remain now... Just a few monolithic places of worship that your 'Druids' are fond of, explained Dixie.

I'm going to have to be careful of what I'm thinking whilst you're a mermaid, said Paul Johnson.

I have always been able to read your thoughts, reminded Dixie, as she turned and smiled at him.

Once inside, they tried to make their way into the main building, right in the centre of this vast underwater Metropolis. Without warning, a spear whooshed past Dixie's head. They both stopped, and realised all about them were Atkinson's elementals – the very type that Dixie had battled so hard against aboard the boat. Dixie swam straight into a crowd of them where the spear came from, beating them with her tail, and slashing at them with her long, extended fingernails. The sea was turning a murky grey colour as she spilled their blood with vicious ferocity. Johnson, without a second's thought, did the same...with one swirl of his body and tail, he sent 30 of them back to the slime that they had crawled out from. But more and more came. Each time they killed an elemental, another two appeared. Dixie screamed out, 'Sentinel!'

Four miles up and a thousand miles away, Gavin stood up and announced he didn't feel well, and was going to lie down.

"The drive down must have given me a headache," he said.

Sensing what was happening, Sarah said, "I will come with you."

The soon-to-be-married couple left the room, and calmly closed the door behind them. As soon as it was closed, Gavin said, "I've got to go!"

"I know – I'm coming with you!" said Sarah, already in Warrior mode.

In a flash of blinding light, they were gone. The door behind where they had been standing opened, and Donald Jackson stood staring, amazed at the speed that his son and soon-to-be daughter-in-law had reached his bedroom.

"I remember a time when I could get you up those stairs that fast!" he said, looking at his wife.

"Donald Jackson, behave yourself! Don't be entertaining silly notions, think of your blood pressure. We don't want any of that nonsense, do we?" said the straight-laced lady sat on the Chesterfield chair.

Again, looking at his wife, he placed his monocle over his left eye and gave her a wink.

"And take that ridiculous thing off of your eye, you silly old man!" said Harriette, picking up her cross-stitch.

Donald relaxed his eye, letting the monocle fall out, wishing Harriette and himself were fit and young again.

Amidst the blood, guts and air bubbles, Gavin and Sarah joined the fray. Sarah grabbed Johnson by the arm and pulled him out of the clutches of several of his fishy foes, then waded into battle. Gavin joined Dixie, who said, *Am I glad to see you, my friend!* Gavin smiled, and as if he was going for a stroll in the park, he drew his mighty sword. The continuous sweeping motion from that great charmed sword, millions of years old, outmatched anything Atkinson's creatures could do. Sarah and Dixie were now seeing off the stragglers, and Johnson looked on in awe as he watched the young Pathologist wield this mighty sword with the ease of a gladiator of old.

*Don't try to work it out, Paul, I don't understand it myself, yet...*whispered Gavin's voice inside the Chief Inspector's head. Soon, the Sentinel's sword was back in its scabbard. Dixie and

Paul were swimming towards the central building, and Gavin and Sarah found themselves back at the bottom of the manor house staircase.

As there were no doors to any of the buildings, they swam straight inside. The long room was ornate, with golden shells and pearls of all sizes. At the far end of the room was a mermaid; her lime-green, tail-length hair floated all about her. Her tail was just like theirs, only more light-sensitive, with thousands of colours – the likes of which Paul had never seen, dancing – within it. Her torso was likened to a teenage boy's, showing slight muscle tone. Her breasts were underdeveloped, but still womanly. Her face could only be described as that of an angel's. She smiled at Dixie and Paul and beckoned to them.

As they drew closer, she raised her right arm, and the now-customary box arose from the ground. Just as it did, through the open window swam a dark figure. It was scaly and had long tentacles, one of which grabbed the box.

The creature made for the door. In an instant a long, green tongue lashed out from the mouth of the vision of beauty that stood before them, wrapped around the body of the thief, and whipped the whole thing back into her mouth. She had just swallowed in one gulp something that was eight feet in length.

The box! screamed Dixie.

The mermaid was now back to how she was when they came in. She smiled and pointed to the floor where her tongue had caught its prey, just as fast as a frog catches a fly. The two Outsiders bowed their heads, picked up the box, and swam out of the building, only to land in the pincers of one of the giant crabs waiting outside. As Johnson felt the pincers cutting into his flesh, he looked at Dixie, who seemed powerless to help.

Did you think it would be so easy to come here, and return alive? They both heard the enormous creature say in Atkinson Senior's voice.

Yes! said Tamara, as her sword's point sliced through the beast's belly from behind and then ripped upwards, tearing the creature in half.

Dressed crab, anyone? she continued.

Dixie and Johnson were relieved to see the mighty Tamara stood there, her blood-covered sword resting on her shoulder and her other hand on her hip, in the classic 'Don't mess with this bitch!' stance.

Would you be so kind as to pass me that box, Mr. Johnson?

Paul Johnson, once again in total awe of this magnificent being, passed her the box.

Nice tail, said Tamara, with a raised eyebrow and a wink...as she disappeared.

Dixie and Paul Johnson held each other's hand and swam to the surface with speed. As they broke the surface, they carried on out of the water into the air, did a double somersault and landed on the deck. Everyone went about their morning strolls on the deck of the Aurora, not even seeing the couple's victorious return.

"Thank you everyone, I'm here all week..." said Johnson, raising his arm in the air.

Dixie just smiled and said, "Come inside...all this has made me horny for you."

In the main office of Atkinson, Dewhirst & Smith, Tamara reappeared, holding the fourth box in her hands. Awaiting her return was John Smith, and also a much stronger-looking Atkinson Junior.

"That was a close one! Your father was expecting us, and ambushed Dixie and Johnson!" said Tamara.

"My father was there?!" exclaimed Atkinson Junior.

"No, not in person, he sent an army of elementals, and that giant crustacean he thinks so much of," she informed.

"I've always hated that thing," said Atkinson Junior.

"Well, you don't have to hate it anymore, because I persuaded it to let Dixie and Johnson go," informed Tamara.

"Clever girl! How did you manage that?" inquired Atkinson Junior.

"Let's just say, he got the point I was making and decided to split."

In the Other Realm, an angry God screamed out in frustration. The howl of discontent vibrated the very walls of the place.

"Something vexes you, Atkinson?" asked Dewhirst with a smirk.

"You know something troubles me!" retorted the angry Deity.

"Maybe you should've left things alone, instead of letting the Otherworldly Beings mate with the primates. Maybe then, you would not be faced with this situation you find yourself in today," replied Dewhirst.

"When I need your advice I will ask for it! Maybe if you weren't so keen on ending your own existence, we would not have been placed in this ridiculous position! I am the supreme God! I will not be moved by you, my idiot son, a mere Listmaker and her snivelling excuse for a Reaper, or a bunch of human beings! Do I make myself clear?" growled the furious Atkinson.

"And what of the Prophecy? Are you above that, too? Oh 'great lord of everything'?" mocked Dewhirst.

"You go too far, old friend. Be mindful of who you are talking to," instructed Atkinson.

"Or you will do precisely what, Atkinson? I have had to put up with you 'Lording it up' for long enough! As for being 'too keen' on ending my own existence...I would rather leap onto an oncoming sword, than spend another second with you!"

"Enough!" interrupted Atkinson.

"Shut up, you stupid old fool! I am your equal! I've only let you go on being the 'supreme God' because it put a stop to your endless, droning monologue! Come on, oh great and powerful God of all things in existence! Bring a lightning bolt from your supreme ass to reduce me to atoms! Maybe, you could sneeze on me, and drown me in the tsunami from your nose! Yes! I am looking forward to the Prophecy coming to fruition – just to see your son drive his sword through your heart and end your reign of terror!"

With that, Dewhirst unceremoniously pushed Atkinson to one side and strode out of the room, leaving Atkinson feeling not quite the God he thought he was.

Back onboard the Aurora, Dixie had led Paul Johnson into the cabin, and had begun ripping away his clothes. It didn't take long to have him totally stripped naked.
"Do the same to me!" she demanded.

Johnson obliged her request, grabbing her dress by the collar, and ripping it away from her body. So intent was he, the dress ripped in two, and he let the two parts fall unnoticed to the floor. She now stood before him in a pair of light violet-coloured lace knickers and matching bra. With one hand, she placed her nimble fingers through the centre front part of her bra, and with the other hand, grasped her knickers – and with one simultaneous movement, she ripped both pieces of underwear away from her body. With her breasts heaving with lust, she pushed Johnson onto the bed and said, "Consider that foreplay."

She then straddled his erect penis and began bouncing up and down upon his lap. This was the first time Paul Johnson had been dominated in bed – and he liked it. He placed his large hands around her breasts and began to squeeze every time her hungry vagina rode his submissive manhood. The thought of being controlled aroused him greatly.
The action of dominating Johnson pushed Dixie's sexual pleasure to a new height as she scraped her nails across his chest. As her arousal increased, so did the pain, as her breasts were now purple from the savage squeezing of Johnson's grip. She gasped,

thinking her nipples would soon explode with ecstasy. Johnson had never been ridden so hard, and his throbbing phallus had never had so much blood pumped into its girth. The pain was excruciatingly pleasurable. As he released his grip on her breasts, his finger marks were clearly indented into her flesh. He took hold of her hair, pulling it, driving his manhood deep into this domineering, masterful woman and then retracted it away from her. He was fired up with adrenalin, and picked his woman up off of him and rose from the bed. It was now time for her to be dominated. Still holding her by her hair he turned her around, let her feet slip to the floor, and then pushed her torso towards the bed, her head and shoulders coming to rest on it but her legs still straight. She rose onto her tiptoes offering herself to him.

He knelt down, lining his face up with her luscious bottom. He pulled her cheeks apart, revealing her womanhood. His tongue first tipped the line between her bum and vagina, producing screams of excitement from his lover. That inquisitive tongue rounded the tiny hole of her bum again and again, causing Dixie to twitch in delight. Beads of perspiration were settling on her brow, and she bit her top lip. Paul Johnson's tongue now entered the Pleasure Dome that his penis had just exited. It was warm, moist and inviting. His tongue now teased her eager clitoris with great accuracy.

Her scream of 'Mister Johnson!!' could be heard all over the ship, it seemed, as he lapped away like the cat that had just found a pot of cream. Johnson did have a very long tongue, and it wasn't long before it found a certain spot in her most intimate of places. All of a sudden, she had to push him away, screaming out very loudly. Accompanying the scream came a whoosh of fluid squirting out from her vagina.

She dug her fingernails into the duvet on the bed as Paul Johnson received an unexpected shower. Rising up, she threw her arms around her lover, kissing his wet face uncontrollably.

"No more..." she whispered in his ear as they sat back on the bed.

Paul Johnson hadn't climaxed, but it was the first time he had caused such a reaction in a woman, and he was pleased. As they both lay naked on the bed, Dixie said, "I wonder what Gavin and Sarah are doing right now."

A long way away in a bedroom in rural England, Sarah muffled a scream of pleasure as she and Gavin climaxed simultaneously.

In the offices of Atkinson, Dewhirst & Smith, Tamara and John Smith were enjoying a cup of tea, discussing that night's list.

"It seems strange how we are just carrying on as normal when we know what is coming," said John Smith.

"No matter what is happening, our work continues. We are unfortunate in the fact that, if we miss one day's reaping, we will never catch up, and the eternal timepiece would forever be wrong. That, my dear friend, is unthinkable...and would bring the end of Humankind. As the battle draws closer, I will make several lists, so whilst we are waging war on Atkinson, you can carry on in the Realm of Death," advised Tamara.

"Won't you need me to help with the battle?" asked John.

"No John. You are needed here, and must carry on the reaping."

"I see...do you mind if I go for a stroll, Tamara?" asked John with an uncertain look in his eye.

"John...do you mean, 'I'm going out Tamara, see to things in my absence,'" corrected Tamara.

John Smith looked puzzled.

"John, you are the boss. You tell me what you are going to do, you don't ask me."

"Oh. I see. In that case, I will be back soon," said John, putting on his jacket.

Passing the elderly gentleman at the desk nearest the door, he said, "I won't be long Mr. Braithwaite, if anyone needs me, put them through to Tamara, would you?"

Braithwaite stood and said, "Of course, Sir."

Once out of the building, John Smith meandered his way through town, thinking about reaping, the war about to unfold and how things had changed for him in the last couple of years. People were passing him by, not knowing they were passing a hooded skeleton with a scythe and hourglass. It wasn't too long before he found himself outside the new hospital building. He walked through the gate and into the hospital. It was visiting time, so nobody asked him why he was there. With no intent for what he was doing, he wandered onto the first ward he came to. The beds were in groups of four to a room. He walked into one of these rooms. There were four women in the beds.

Three of the women were just lying there asleep. The fourth, Jasmine Lester, looked straight at him and asked in a strong West-Indian accent, "Who have you come for? For I am not ready to meet you."

John Smith looked shocked and said, "Excuse me?"

"You are Walking Death and you have come to collect a soul – but whose soul is it, Reaper?" continued the woman.

"I think you have the wrong man!" said a startled Smith.

"You are no man," replied the woman.

"Good day, madam," said Smith, as he quickly made an exit.

"I will await the Goddess' call," said the woman.

John Smith was shocked, and did not understand how she knew what he was...and he also didn't understand her last statement.

He left the ward. Making his way into the corridor, he saw a sign for Pathology. Knowing that was where Gavin Jackson worked, he made his way there. He stepped into the Pathology Department, which at first looked empty, but it wasn't long before a young man came to greet him.

"Can I help you?" asked Tom Harper.

"Is Gavin Jackson here?" replied John Smith.

"I'm afraid not. Is there anything that I can help you with? I'm Mr. Jackson's assistant."

"I thought Sarah was his assistant?" said Smith.

Tom gave a wry smile, and said, "No, I'm his assistant. Her job is to stress me out...which, I might add, she is very proficient at."

"Ahhh...you must be Tom Harper!" said John Smith.

"I am indeed! But you have me at a disadvantage, Sir!"

"Sorry, I'm John Smith. I'm a friend of Gavin and Sarah."

"In that case, it's a pleasure to meet you, Mr. Smith. But you are perspiring...perhaps a drink of water?" Tom said with a smile.

"That would be wonderful, I've just had a shock," John replied.

"In that case, step into the office, and make yourself comfortable. I shall put the kettle on, a cup of tea fixes anything," said Tom Harper.

John made himself comfortable in Gavin Jackson's office, and it wasn't too long before Tom was back with a tray of tea and a plate of digestive biscuits.

"You're looking a tad better now, John...may I call you John?" enquired Tom, as he passed John Smith a cup of tea.

"Of course you can, Tom," he answered.

"I'm sorry Gavin isn't here for you, I hope it wasn't important...I can get in touch with him if it is," offered Tom.

"No thank you, there won't be any need for that – nice cup of tea, by the way – just what I needed," answered John.

There was a moment of uneasy silence, which Tom broke by saying, "So...what caused you to be so distressed when you arrived?"

"Oh yes, that...well, I was in the hospital, and a woman mistook me for someone else and it all got a bit emotional...if you know what I mean," said John.

"Were you visiting someone?" asked Tom.

"Err, no...I was just...well, to tell the truth, I don't know why I was there...I was just having a stroll to clear my head and somehow found myself there," explained John.

"Maybe it was fate that took you there...you might be a long-lost relative of the person you saw. Do you...believe in fate, John?" asked Tom.

"I believe we all have a given time to live...if that's what you mean by fate," answered John.

"In my job, I'm dissuaded from believing in certain set lengths of life – and if you only knew about life and death, John, you would know what I mean," said Tom.

"Of course, I bow to your superior knowledge of the subject," said a smiling John.

"You're Gavin's accountant, aren't you?" enquired Tom.

"Indeed I am."

"I've been thinking about investing a little sum of money – should I come and see you for advice?" asked Tom.

"Well...I'm not really a financial advisor, as such, I'm an accountant...but I can certainly give you a push in the right direction. But for now, I have a busy night ahead of me, so I'd better be on my way."

The two men shook hands, and John Smith left the Pathology Department of the hospital, making his way back to his office. Tom Harper had enjoyed his 20 minutes with Sarah's friend, and thought, maybe his life shouldn't be all about work...and he really did need to sort out his finances...

Chapter Eight

In a Realm of neither Existence nor Death stood an incomplete being – a being hated by Humanity, cast out by his father, and loved by one. In the Realm of Death there was a Reaper who still didn't trust him. On the Plane of Existence a group of Warriors and a human were working towards his imminent return.

Atkinson Junior, who up until his previous Administration almost a quarter of a century past had lived the charmed life of a God with everything at his fingertips, was now cast adrift in a strange limbo between worlds. He was at the moment powerless, whilst his body was incomplete and at the mercy of anything – God or friend – that had the power to find him in that dark, foreboding place.

Every time he connected with Tamara, to some degree, he gave away his vulnerable position. In his head, he heard Tamara's sweet voice...*Be patient, my love – do not present yourself before me anymore – when you do that, your position is unsafe. There are only three more boxes to retrieve...and then you are whole again, and ready to take your rightful place as the one to claim your father's position.*

You are right, Tamara, telepathy is the only way we should make contact. I know I can trust you – but I am unsure about those around you. I put Smith through a lot...and I tried to kill the rest of them.

*You tried to kill me too, remember? In fact, you did...*reminded Tamara.

Yes I did; but I knew they would regenerate you...I love you, said Atkinson Junior.

Don't think of these things now – once we have you back, you can start building bridges with the others, comforted Tamara.

Wait! Tamara...there's someone here! I can hear them walking towards me...who is it, Tamara?

At that very point, the telepathic link between the two was severed. Tamara stood up from her chair just as John Smith stepped back into the office.

"Tamara, what's wrong!?" asked John, running to catch her as she fainted. He caught her just in time. Easing her back into her chair, he brought a glass of water to her. She sipped the drink, the moisture clinging to her plump lips, making them glisten and shine. She opened her eyes and looked at him, and then shouted, "Atkinson!"

"No, Tamara, it's me – John Smith!"

"I think Atkinson is in trouble! I had a telepathic link with him and it ended suddenly, just as someone was walking towards him!" exclaimed Tamara in an uncommonly nervous voice.

"Only I can be in there," said Smith.

"Yes, John, but you aren't in there, are you?" retorted Tamara, who then stopped, looked at John and said, "How did you know where he was?"

"I don't know...it just came to me the first time he appeared here," answered Smith.

"Oh no...if you knew, that means we all know, and that includes..."

"Atkinson and Dewhirst," he interrupted.

Back in that strange realm, a ghostly apparition dragged a sword along the floor, its point raising sparks, moving ever closer to Atkinson Junior. Atkinson recognized the sword; it was his father's mighty broadsword – but he did not recognize his would-be assassin.

John Smith ran back to the old door behind his desk, quickly passing through into the Realm of Death, his sword now in his hand. He moved with speed to where Atkinson Junior sat, passing through the portal that placed him in the same realm as Atkinson Junior and his assailant. Raising his reaping sword, he charged at the entity about to terminate Atkinson Junior. The beast raised both arms with its hands tightly gripping the handle of Atkinson's father's sword, about to deliver its killing blow. Smith lashed across its arms from behind, removing them at the elbow. Within the same movement, he drew the sword back and plunged it deep between the beast's shoulder blades; with all his might, he then ripped it through the top part of the thing's body and head, splitting its top half in two. As the creature fell to the ground, the sword, still clenched in its severed hands, clattered onto the floor, illuminating the darkness with sparks. Atkinson Junior shouted, "Grab that sword!" John Smith dove onto it and picked it up just before it would have disappeared with the beast that had wielded it.

"Well done, John!" gasped a very relieved Atkinson Junior.

"I didn't know you knew my first name!" said Smith in surprise.

"I didn't think it would be you coming to save me!" replied Atkinson Junior.

"Tamara will have to find a new place for you, now that they know where you are," said John.

"Very true," replied Atkinson Junior. "I do have an idea, but it will require you to be with me until I am ready to return."

"I was thinking along the same lines myself. Follow me back into the Realm of Death," said Smith.

"Once you are in there nobody else can enter. As I am in shadow and not physical, I can be there with you. Here is the thing, though – as soon as you leave, my father will take your place there as there is another portal in the Other Realm – and that will be Game Over," informed Atkinson Junior.

"What about the reaping?" asked Smith.

"While you are in here, the timepiece stops. No matter how long you reside within this dark chamber, only twenty or so minutes will pass on the Plane of Existence. That will work to our advantage, as you will not have to leave to pick up a list."

The telepathic link was now working again between the two Reapers and Tamara, so she was privy to the whole conversation, and for the moment, the immediate danger had passed.

At a run-down farm in the mid-Western quarter of Russia, a silo door opened in the ground, much to the shock of the two operators 170 feet below the surface. All of the sirens were wailing, and the lights were flashing on their control panel. The launch system had begun. Vladimir Borgeski, who was the man in charge of the silo, looked at his young counterpart, and both men readied their launch keys. They checked the time, inserted the keys, and simultaneously twisted one-quarter turn to the right. In flashing red numbers, the console clock's glowing baleful face had begun the sixty-second countdown to launch, and the beginning of what they hoped would be the saviour of the Earth.

"It is good that the first missile to save the planet is from Mother Russia," said Vladimir, now standing to attention and saluting.

Five, four, three, two, one...the missile blasted off, left the silo, and gained speed as it shot up into the atmosphere. The two men monitored its progress as it left the stratosphere and headed for space, with a long journey ahead of it. It blasted off right on the time it had been programmed to start its journey. The two men congratulated each-other on a job well done. This scene was now taking place all over the world, one after another, with no one knowing they were all setting off at the right time, but one day too early. Because of the complexity of the launches, NASA had not given specific days – just the signal when it was time to launch.

At NASA, Tom Hackett, one of the scientists assigned to tracking the missiles once they were launched, noticed what looked like a problem. During a routine check of the first twelve missile launches and current trajectories, he calculated that all the missiles would merge a full 24 hours before they should, effectively all passing each other and heading off into space. He contacted the flight director Jed Jeffries, and passed on his findings. JJ, as he was known to the rest of the Mission Control Team, left his position and walked over to Tom Hackett's console. Covering his microphone, he said to Tom, "Could you run that by me again?"

"I have checked and double-checked, JJ, they have all taken off 24 hours too early...and the rest are still blasting off all over the world.

"My god! We must stop the launches!" yelled the director, making his way back to his post.

"Listen up everyone! We have a situation here! Either we have our arithmetic wrong, which I doubt very much, A launch problem, or..." JJ hesitated for a moment, and then continued. "Or...the launch data has been deliberately changed...because all of these launches are a day too early. I need the stop codes sent out! I want these launches stopped while we figure out the problem!"

It was Mark Barrett's console that was in charge of the override, but try as he may, he could not gain entry into the system. "JJ...my codes are not working! I cannot initiate the override! All my codes have been changed!" explained the worried controller.

"Who changed it, and why!?" demanded the Flight Director.

"I'm efforting that right now, Sir," said Barrett.

After what seemed like an eternity, but in fact was only 45 seconds, he said, "Ken Jones."

"Get him in here...fast!" shouted Jed Jeffries.

From another console, Ken Jones' replacement said, "He isn't in today, JJ...he didn't turn up for work this morning."

"I want him here...in fifteen minutes!" Turning to the security officer by the door, he said, "Make it happen!"

The security officer quickly turned and left the room. Not much time had passed before the same security officer rang back, and informed JJ that Ken Jones was dead – and by the look of the empty whiskey bottle and tablet containers, he had taken his own life. The flight director slammed his fists onto his console...but then regained his composure and said, "Find that new password! Stop everything else! Just get into that programme!"

The controllers gathered into small groups and began the arduous job of retracing Ken Jones' steps on his computer in an effort to find this new password.

Back at Gavin Jackson's parents' house, the soon-to-be-wed couple stepped back into the drawing room.

"Hello you two!" said Donald Jackson with a beaming smile.

"Are you feeling better, son?" asked his mother.

"I am indeed...and feeling rather hungry, too!" said Gavin.

"Excellent! I will let Jarvis know we are ready for dinner!" said his father.

Harriette Jackson, Gavin and Sarah made their way into the rather grand dining room, soon joined by the master of the house. Donald Jackson sat at the head of the 12 foot-long Italian inlaid ornate dining table, his wife sitting at the opposite end. The young lovers sat opposite each other halfway down the table. It wasn't long before Jarvis and Alice brought in the first course of wild game soup – a rich concoction of grouse and quail in a decadent broth. It wasn't to Sarah's taste, but she wasn't going to upset anyone by not eating it. The other three loved it. After the soup tureen and the bowls were removed, the second course made its way to the table – roast beef with minted potatoes, carrots and baby asparagus.

Again, Sarah wasn't too sure about the asparagus, having never seen it before. She dug her fork into one of the tender spears, and holding it up asked very politely, "What is this?"

"That, my dear, is asparagus, have you never tried it before?" asked Harriette.

"I've never seen it before," she said smilingly.

"Go on girl…just take a bite! You may be surprised!" encouraged Donald.

She placed the tip of a spear into her mouth and took a bite. Her eyes opened wide, and a huge smile lit up her small face. The rest of the family chuckled at Sarah's expression and everyone tucked into their lovely meals. After the main course came the profiteroles, another first for Sarah, but again, a welcome one. Gavin looked at this wonderful girl across the table with chocolate sauce on her lips and smiled.

"Tricky little buggers, those profiteroles!" laughed Donald.

"Language, Donald!" said Harriette.

Gavin and Sarah laughed.

With the meal over, the family rose from the table and made their way back into the drawing room. It wasn't long before Jarvis entered the room with a tray of tea, and an assortment of minty chocolates.

Sarah stood up and said, "Shall I be mum?" Picking up the teapot, she poured the tea into the little china cups. Gavin's mother beamed as she was handed the first cup, and said, "Thank you child, what a lovely girl you are. Now…do tell me why you have all of these sketches on your arms."

"Sketches, old girl? Those are tattoos!" boomed Gavin's father.

"You mean they are…permanent?" croaked Harriette with a gasp.

"Harriette!" exclaimed Donald Jackson, still desperately trying to fit his rather large forefinger through the tiny aperture of the bone china handle of his cup.

"It's okay – I know to some people they aren't nice, and I understand that. I have had a very bad life you see...and these tattoos remind me that it hasn't been my fault. I had no one to turn to, and I didn't have a proper family to help me work things out. As the tattooist was putting a new picture on me, I was telling myself it was all going to work out. In a way, I was sharing the story of my life. I am not a bad person for having ink on my body, it was just my way of coping."

Harriette took a sip of her tea, looked at her soon-to-be daughter-in-law, and said, "I'm sorry my dear, I was insensitive. I never looked at it that way. Do accept my apologies...you must show them off to the world! And if anyone has anything negative to say about them, I will deal with them!" said the Chairwoman of the Allerton Chapel branch of the Women's Institute...and the newest champion for tattoos.

In his bedroom, working hard on his computer, Jeff Clarke read his would-be Pulitzer-prize-winning 'story of all stories'. He thought about the fights he had had with Donald Steele over it...the time it had taken to write...the friends he had lost whilst gathering information for it. He then thought how pointless it all was, for no matter the outcome of what was on the horizon, no one would ever read it.

He looked about the room he had spent most of his teenage years in...the poster of the Fantastic Four on the windowed wall. Spiderman and Superman adorned the wall space above his bed. Most of the third wall was taken up by the door and wardrobe, and a very large poster of The Hulk was proudly displayed on the fourth. Picking up a wooden-framed 10 x 8" photograph of Cindy off his bedside cabinet, he said, "You were always my Wonder Woman."

"I hope I still am," said Cindy's angelic voice at his side.

Jeff's head spun round to the side, and on seeing her sweet face, he said, "No, you are my forever angel – and you are just in time to witness a ceremony." He highlighted the story of stories in blue, and then depressed the backspace button on his keyboard.

"You gave Mr. Steele ulcers over that story! It's a good thing he is not here to witness what you just did!" said Cindy with a giggle.

"I know I did, and at times, I feel sad about that now," said Jeff.

"Don't think about that now...we have an eternity to look forward to," said Cindy.

"I know that...and now I understand it's what I was born to do," said Jeff, looking at the sword against the wall by the Hulk.

Cindy leaned over and kissed him. "Remember, what you have to do to Dewhirst is kind of ceremonial, and – it is what he wants."

"I know, that's the way I'm looking at it. Tamara explained all of that, and I'm cool with it. I know that if I don't do this, the world as we know it could disappear," said Jeff.

Cindy smiled at him and said, "I will go for a while now...and I suggest the time between now and when you are needed you spend with your mother, for when I gain you forever, she will lose you."

"I hadn't thought of that!" said Jeff, wearing a thoughtful expression.

The Realm of Death is a dark, foreboding place, where no one in their right mind would want to stay. But at the moment, it was sanctuary to Atkinson Junior, and a self-imposed prison for John Smith. In this strange realm with Mortal Cords emanating from every angle, the two sat talking about how they had reached this point in their existences.

"Why did you need a surrogate?" enquired John.

"It was so the situation we find ourselves in today couldn't happen. My father wanted to keep total control of my existence, so I wasn't given the same status as they...and for me to exist at all, I needed a human counterpart."

"But it has happened," said Smith.

"Yes, it has. This is because of what happened last year."

"In what way did that change things?" asked John.

"When my father reanimated my dead body and chained me to the wall, it changed my status. I was hoping for this to happen. I was also hoping that my father didn't realise what the outcome of his actions would be. Then I had the realisation they had not tightened my bonds...which made me think he was testing me. With that in mind, I knew I had to go through the whole thing again to gain his trust, and prove my hatred of the human race mirrored his," instructed Atkinson.

"So you chose two painful deaths and decapitation to prove to your father his way of going about things would carry on?"

"Yes. I was prepared to be nasty through my follow-on Administrations to attain this end."

"Are you referring to the Prophecy?" asked Smith.

"The Prophecy had not entered my mind...until Jeff Clarke joined the fray. As I already had set things in motion, I couldn't stop them."

"Jeff Clarke?" said Smith.

"I knew he was the other one who could make the Prophecy occur. I also knew I had to keep up the pretence with my father, or he would have just ended Humankind there and then. I had to hope he lived through the devastation, and beyond. That's why I made you fetch him to my...sorry, your office, the day the gas main blew under the newspaper building," said Atkinson.

"Have you been behind all the decisions I have made since becoming Reaper?"

"In the early part of your Administration, yes, just as my father did with me. You see, in this company, we cannot make mistakes. Our 'employees' cannot go to arbitration about how we run things...and our 'clients' certainly have no say in our actions. So, every single action we take must be the right one. And do remember, you are only the fourth being to hold this position – and that is how it will stay if all goes to plan."

"What about Jeff? Doesn't that make it five beings?"

"He will be the Scribe. It is what he was born to do."

"So just you and I reaping, then?" asked Smith.

"Yes, and the fact that we have different sexual orientations makes me happy," said Atkinson Junior.

"Why? I thought you didn't like gay men."

"First and foremost, I don't share Tamara. And secondly, I am not that being who did those awful crimes – it was all part of a bigger plan."

John Smith nodded his head and said, "Well, here's to new beginnings! I will expect you to shake my hand when you are whole again."

"I look forward to that day," agreed Atkinson Junior.

In the Other Realm, thunder and lightning were crashing and flashing all around. Elementals were running for cover, as bolt after bolt of electricity streaked from Atkinson's vicious fingers. His anger grow with the latest defeat, which had quickly followed his attempt to stop Dixie and Johnson retrieving his son's body part. Dewhirst calmly walked into the chamber strewn with dead elementals, looked about at the mayhem, and said, "Have you lost something, Atkinson?"

"Do not vex me this day, Dewhirst!" growled his partner.

"I'm simply asking a valid question...it's just, I have a sword, and I wondered if you fancied sparring...since we might be having to use them soon?" said Dewhirst with a smile.

"You don't know one end of a sword from the other, you foolish old man!" said Atkinson.

At those words, Dewhirst's sword was unsheathed, its point at Atkinson's throat. "Still young enough to catch you off guard – and at least I do have a sword!" spat Dewhirst, his nose touching Atkinson's.

Dewhirst retracted the blade and threw it on the floor. His intense stare glared into the black eyes of his one-time friend. He turned and walked away, saying, "And stop all that ridiculous noise."

Atkinson's anger grew more intense than ever before, as he shouted, "You will see! There will be no prophecy for you, my friend! Maybe we cannot kill each other — but we can't join someone else's fight, either!"

Dewhirst walked away and under his breath, he said, "I already have."

Back at NASA Mission Control, Flight Director Jed Jeffries had waited long enough. Calling out to his controllers he said, "Why do we not have the new access code?"

Although the best brains on the planet were working on the problem, it was in fact the very finest brain on the planet that had changed the code, and his was the only brain that couldn't be called upon. The answer JJ received was not the one he wanted.

"Listen up, everyone! If we can't find this goddam code — let's start sending word out to the silos for them to manually stop these things from lift-off — or we are not going to have any left to use!" said the Flight Director.

A single solemn controller hit his microphone button and nervously said, "We can't do that, JJ."

"What?!" exclaimed the Flight Director.

"We didn't have time to install a manual override...it wasn't a contingency we thought we would need... also, we are talking about a whole load of silos here, JJ."

"Alternatives, people! Give me alternatives!"

"We could try individually getting in touch with them..." said a different controller.

"That would take forever! There are thousands of them!" exclaimed another.

"We have over a thousand people on standby – let's get them in on it!" said JJ.

"It's still going to take too long...half of the missiles are already en route," said yet another controller.

"We have to do something!" shouted a despondent JJ.

There was a crackle in his earpiece, and the word, "Flight", followed it.

"Yes?" replied JJ.

"From my console, I believe the mission is over. We have already lost half of our fire power – the rest will have shot into space before we can do anything about it. If we had found out sooner – maybe, just maybe, we may have saved enough missiles... but we would not have had time to do the reset. As I said, from my seat...the mission is over."

JJ sat back in his chair and put his head in his hands. He said in a slightly muffled voice, "Thank you, ladies and gentlemen...the mission is over."

He rose from his chair of authority with none of his usual flair, walked solemnly to the door, and entered the room of his superior. His boss was sitting at his desk, and had been throughout the crisis. Walking up to the desk he said, "You had better ring the President and tell him Armageddon is upon us."

Chapter Nine

Paul Johnson stood on the port side of the Aurora, staring out to sea. Being forward of the bridge, he could see the bow waves rolling away from the ship. His thoughts were no longer of home or police work...they were not even about reaping, or quests. They centred on something that had become the most important part of his life – Dixie. He had fallen head-over-heels in love with this wonderful being. He totally admired her wit, her strength, her femininity...even the tiny little mole she had just above her left eyebrow.

He dare not allow himself to think of the future they might have, because there were too many chips stacked up against them as a couple. The fact that she wasn't human was one obstacle, and the fact that if they ever had an argument, she could tear his arms right off his body was another. He chuckled to himself as he thought being unfaithful would certainly be out of the question. Yes, this...whatever...she was...was now a big part of his life, and if he had started this quest not really caring if it was successful or not, or for that matter if he lived or perished – he was now in a different mind-set. He just wanted it to be over, and to be back on dry land with his new soul mate.

"There is a good way to go before that happens, Paul..."
Johnson spun around, and the beautiful vision of Tamara was there.

"They are just my personal thoughts for what might be," said Paul Johnson.

"There were no promises at the start of the quest that you, or anyone, would return – and things have gotten decidedly harder for you both now that Atkinson is onto you."

"I am aware of all this – but one can hope," said Chief Inspector Paul Johnson.

"Indeed we can, and in fact, we must. It's the only thing we have until Atkinson Junior returns," whispered Tamara.

"You haven't come here just to spoil my daydream – what is the problem?" asked Johnson.

"We came very close to losing Atkinson Junior a short while ago. It was the quick actions of John Smith that saved him. Smith has also managed to procure Atkinson Senior's sword. This is the first stroke of luck we have had, because Atkinson's immense power is lessened by not having his sword. So, for the first time in this conflict, we have gained some power. It's only a little, but it just might give us an edge," informed Tamara.

"Well done, John Smith!" said Johnson.

"Remember Paul, be extra vigilant...and watch out for each-other. There are three more boxes to retrieve – be very careful – you are not safe until you are back on the boat," said Tamara as she disappeared.

Rolling over the starboard safety rail, a low mist replaced the mighty Warrior.

*Once more unto the breach, dear friends, once more...*was the dramatic thought that entered Paul Johnson's mind

It was now evening in the country residence of Gavin Jackson's parents, and all talk was either of the wedding, or the following day's visit to see the happy couple's new apartment. No matter how Harriette tried, she could not gain information from Sarah about the elusive wedding dress. Gavin and Donald's discussion had now turned to the main difference between the beautiful

Jaguar under the tarpaulin parked outside, and the equivalent sports cars of today.

"There is something regal about an aged Jaguar," remarked Donald.

"Agreed, father!" endorsed Gavin.

"Just listen to those two — they're like two little boys judging their favourite toys!" quipped the lady of the house.

Apartments, weddings and Jaguars continued until late into the night, with apartments winning by a narrow margin. After a nightcap, the Jackson family made their way up the immense central staircase to their separate respective bedrooms.

Below stairs, Jarvis, Mrs. Jarvis the cook, and Alice Jarvis the chambermaid were having their late-night hot chocolate. Most of their evening, too, had been taken up by the up-and-coming nuptials of Gavin and Sarah, when all of a sudden there was a knock on the kitchen interior door. Jarvis immediately rushed to answer.

"Miss Sarah! Do excuse my slovenliness!" exclaimed Jarvis as he pinched up his tie.

Sarah placed her hands on his own industrious hands and stopped them.

"Mr. Jarvis — please don't do that for me — I am in your part of the house now, so there is no need for you to be uncomfortable," comforted Sarah.

"How can I be of service, madam?" asked Jarvis.

"Gavin is asleep in the next room, and I was lonely in my room and couldn't sleep, so could I sit with you for a while?"

"Of course you can, Miss Sarah! Quickly Alice, move over and let me sit next to you so that Miss Sarah can have my seat."

"Please Mr. Jarvis, let me sit next to Sarah — I don't want to take your seat."

"As you wish, Miss Sarah. Alice, let the Miss sit next to you."

Alice shuffled her bum across the wooden bench and made way for Sarah.

"Would Miss care for a hot chocolate?" invited Jarvis.

"Ooohhh...I would love one!" Sarah answered eagerly.

After the beverage arrived, Sarah said, "I need to ask you a question, Mr. Jarvis."

"Indeed, madam?"

"I want to ask if Alice can be my bridesmaid."

Alice's face lit up...no one had ever asked her to be a bridesmaid before!

"Certainly not, Miss Sarah! The lady of the house would never sanction such a thing!" gasped Jarvis.

Sarah's eyes began to well with tears, and Alice's bottom lip began to quiver.

"It's not up to Gavin's mother who I have as my bridesmaid! I only have two girlfriends in the whole wide world! One of them is my sister, and the other is Alice. My sister is far too busy to be my bridesmaid – so if my only other girlfriend can't do it – I will have nobody!" said Sarah, bursting into tears.

"Please don't cry, Miss...why don't you ask the lady of the house on the morrow...she might say yes," said Jarvis, not believing a word of what he had just said.

"Ok, I will!" said Sarah, as she leant over and dried Alice's eyes, then kissed her on the cheek. On standing up, Sarah said, "Goodnight, Mr. Jarvis, goodnight, Mrs. Jarvis...goodnight Alice." She sadly returned to her room. Sarah took off her dressing gown, picked up Miss Behavin' her plush hamster, and cuddled her tight as she began to cry herself to sleep.

In the room next door, Gavin heard her sobs and quickly made his way to her.

"Whatever is the matter, Sarah?"

Sarah told Gavin what had just transpired, and Gavin said, "If you want little Alice to be your bridesmaid, bridesmaid she will be. I will speak to Mother after breakfast.

"Ahhh, thank you Gavin! But, you have to do it when she's 'on the morrow'... that's what Mr. Jarvis said."

"I will see to it that she is," said Gavin with a smile as he gave his betrothed a comforting kiss.

Sarah smiled sweetly, cuddled Miss Behavin', and fell fast asleep.

The mist had now engulfed the Aurora, and out of their cabin door came Dixie and the Chief Inspector.

"Ready yourself, Paul!"

Just as those words escaped her lips, a cannonball flashed across the deck, just missing Johnson.

"Here we go again!" shouted Johnson as he stood at the wheel of the 'Man-O-War' galleon.

As he looked starboard, a pirate ship with tattered, battle-weary sails and a crew to match sailed up alongside.

"Keep a sharp eye, crew!" shouted Captain Johnson.

"Keep a sharp eye!" repeated the parrot perched upon his shoulder.

Dixie took the dagger from her clenched teeth, her breasts trying to burst out from her bar-wench dress, and said with a laugh, "Are all your imaginary thoughts clichés?

Johnson gave a hearty, "Hahaaa, Jim Lad!" followed by a, "Splice the main brace!" Then he said, "What is a main brace, anyway?"

Dixie just laughed, shook her head, then put the dagger back in her mouth and grabbed a rope. Johnson leapt down to where she was, grabbed the rope with her, then they both swashbuckled their way onto the other ship, just like they were in a Jonny Depp movie.

With John Smith's next list completed, her earlier dealings with Johnson over for now, and her phone to the Other Realm definitely disconnected, Tamara had the first 'me-time' she had had since before the Town Hall Tower incident – and boy was she going to enjoy it. Throwing a long coat over her shoulders, she passed Braithwaite, saying, "Get in touch with me if the world is coming to an end – absolutely nothing else!"

The elderly gentleman nodded his head as she left the building.

Upon reaching her beautifully-kept apartment, she clapped her hands together, and her personal elementals all disappeared. Just as soon as Tamara had made the decision in her mind to come home, the elementals had made sure her apartment was in top shape. They ran her a bath with the richest of oils, and on top of the bubbles, rose petals floated. At the side of the very large stand-alone bath was an ice bucket containing a bottle of Dom Perignon, and a small table holding a single rose and a champagne glass.

Walking into the hallway, she let her coat fall to the ground, unfastening her beautiful necklace and letting it fall, as well. Taking hold of the bottom of her chiffon top, with her crossed hands she lifted it over her head. As she was still walking she let it drag behind her for a while, and then released it to the ground. Climbing up the stairs, she stepped out of her tight pencil skirt, placing her right foot on the next step and then exiting the bespoke garment. With one hand behind her back, her nimble fingers persuaded her bra loose. Just before entering, she paused at the door to the bathroom. Placing her fingers in each side of her knickers, she eased them down to her knees, then bent forward, sliding them off her legs and stepping free of their confinement. As she rose, the undergarment dangled from her fingertips; she then let it fall to the ground, joining the rest of her abandoned attire.

Twisting her hair in one hand, she clasped it in place with a beautiful jewel-studded pearly clip, and then eased herself into the waiting tub of luxury. A snap of her fingers, and the lights dimmed. A second snap, and Mozart's 'Magic Flute' wafted through the sound system. She lay back, and for a short time, she was just an ordinary girl in a bath, relaxing.

Whilst relaxing in the tub, this ordinary girl's clothing worth a small fortune, was being silently cleared away by her many housekeeping elementals.

Dixie and Johnson both landed on the deck together, and began the now-customary fight, and as with other such bouts on this quest, they outmatched their opponents easily. Amidst the cracking timbers, cannon fire, smoke and strewn bodies they battled on long and hard, finally claiming the pirate ship as their own. In a chest just before the main mast was the treasure Captain Paul Johnson, the feared Captain of the Seven Seas had come for, but as he picked it up a shot rang out from the rigging and a bullet with his name on it hurtled towards its target.

Back at Tamara's apartment, her bath time was interrupted, as a blood-stained chest containing Atkinson Junior's body part arrived unannounced.

At the scene of the battle stood Johnson with tears in his eyes, and the lifeless body of his beloved Dixie lying limp in his arms, a blood-stained bullet hole in her chest from where she had leapt in front of him to take his bullet. He fell to his knees, clutching the girl he wanted to spend the rest of his life with in his arms, and screamed out loud. When the scream was over, he was back in his cabin upon the Aurora...alone.

Within the Realm of Death, Atkinson Junior stood to his feet. "He has the fifth piece!" he exalted.

"That's great! Only two more and you'll be back!" rejoiced Smith.

"But all is not well...one of them has fallen...it's the being from the Other Realm. Tamara will have to replace her before the next part of the quest," said Atkinson Junior.

Tamara felt a jolt, and found herself standing in a dark room, naked and dripping wet. A cloaked figure came from the shadows and said, "This is unexpected, Listmaker...what do you propose to do?"

"I will take care of it – I will get him another Warrior," answered Tamara.

"And what good is another Warrior when he has bonded with the one he had?"

"I know Great One...but I didn't foresee this..." explained Tamara.

"Enough of making this easy for the human, with all this drama attached to such a simple undertaking!"

"I'd hoped using his past thoughts would make him want to succeed more," said Tamara with her head down.

"Clearly it has not. Get this job done! I want no more of this nonsense! Your very presence is teetering on a knife's edge! I want no more mistakes! By the way, Listmaker...you may use this," he said, releasing Dixie from under his robe. Dewhirst then disappeared.

Tamara found herself back in the bathtub...and Dixie found herself back in time by several minutes.

Dixie and Johnson both landed on the deck together, and began the now-customary fight. As with other such bouts on this quest, they outmatched their opponents easily. Amidst the cracking timbers, cannon fire, smoke and strewn bodies, they battled long and hard, and finally claimed the pirate ship as their own. In a chest just before the main mast was the treasure Johnson had come for. As he picked it up, Dixie hurled her knife right past his head and into the heart of a would-be assassin nestling in the rigging. Johnson ran to Dixie and whisked her off her feet, twirling her round in a love embrace. Dixie was crying as he looked into her eyes, and said, "What's wrong?"

She kissed him hard on the mouth and burst into peals of teary laughter. "I nearly lost you there for a moment! But we are together again."

In her bathtub, Tamara was sitting upright, her arms clenched around her knees, deep in thought. She knew going so directly against Atkinson Senior, as Dewhirst had just done, would have taken much of his power and left him vulnerable. Should Atkinson Senior find out what had happened, he would do everything in his power to make The End his new reality before his son was ready to face him.

Her fears were realized, because Atkinson Senior had been waiting for his friend on his return. In the Other Realm, Dewhirst lay battered and bleeding on the floor. Atkinson, his hands dripping with blood and raging at his one-time friend, had landed punch after punch. The tired old Deity was left with nothing to defend himself with, and offered no resistance to Atkinson's onslaught.

"Before I beat you into Oblivion, I will show you the destruction of Humankind. I will bring the asteroid crashing down on the Earth right now!"

Atkinson raised his hands into the air and began to chant. Although battered and beaten, Dewhirst began to laugh at his partner.

"Are you demented, you stupid old fool?" asked Atkinson, as he temporarily halted his actions.

Dewhirst laughed louder, and said, "Whoooooo...whoooo..." He raised his arms weakly and repeated Atkinson's moves in a ghostly manner. "I am going to wave my hands in the air...and end allll things...because I can!"

"You dare mock my actions?!" growled Atkinson.

"You are a coward, Atkinson. You are ending things not for your hatred of Humankind – you are scared of that idiot son of yours. You dare not meet him in combat...because he is more powerful than you."

"I am not scared of anything!" exclaimed Atkinson.

"In that case, you are a bigger fool than I thought...and you waited until I could not fight back before you dare confront me...that's how I know you are frightened to face your son in battle! In my book, that makes you a simple coward!" scorned Dewhirst.

The chatter of elementals could be heard all over the realm, and the word 'coward' was ringing loudly in Atkinson's ears. Atkinson lowered his arms and said, "Okay, Dewhirst...what would you have me do to prove you wrong?"

"Hold back the asteroid one day...and face your son."

"Do you think me stupid, you old fool? No, I won't play into your hands – I will bring the damned thing nearer by a day. My son had better quicken his pace, if he wants to meet me!" said Atkinson, as a mere wave of his hand brought the enormous asteroid exactly 24 hours closer to Earth.

Atkinson walked out of the room feeling superior, having outwitted the old fool on the ground. By knowing Atkinson would do the exact opposite of what he asked, the 'old fool' on the ground had just put all of NASA's missiles back on track. A multitude of elementals ran to Dewhirst, passing into him their life force – sacrificing themselves to his regeneration. Dewhirst stood back up on his feet, with a wry smile on his old face.

At NASA, although the mission was over, the inquest into its failure was still going on. Tom Hackett had left the huddle of controllers he had been working with and returned to his terminal, sitting back down at his desk. He was just about to turn off his small section of Mission Control, where he had sat for many years, through many missions, when something on the screen caught his eye. Without saying anything, he plugged his headset back in and pulled his swivel chair into the desk and began calculating. After re-checking his results twice, he looked back over his shoulder to where JJ was tidying up his papers and placing them in his briefcase. Very quietly, he said, "JJ..."

Jed Jefferies glanced up from what he had been doing and said, "Yes?"

Tom motioned him over to his terminal.

"What's going on?" asked JJ.

"I need you to listen to what I have to say very carefully," said Tom.

"Go ahead," replied JJ.

"I don't know how...but the asteroid is going to hit in three days."

"Four days," corrected JJ.

"Three days," repeated Tom, showing JJ his screen.

"I don't understand...how can it possibly be three days? Are you trying to tell me this asteroid has leapt a full 24 hours ahead of itself?" said JJ, scratching his head.

"That is exactly what I'm saying," said Tom Hackett calmly.

"Put it up on the main screen...you've got a glitch on your terminal."

Tom depressed a key on his computer, and the flight plan of the asteroid that was on his screen now illuminated the large front screen of Mission Control, clearly showing that its path had moved a full 24 hours closer.

Everybody in the room was now looking at the screen agog.

"Were the first readings wrong? Were we out by a day?" asked one of the Controllers.

"That can be the only answer," said Tom.

"But we all checked your conversions," said JJ.

"And we were all wrong. I'm glad it isn't just me who needs to go back to school," said Tom.

"Everybody return to your terminals and re-check this!" said the Flight Director.

Like a flash, everybody was back at their respective places, slide rules in hand. It wasn't very long before each and every controller had given the new data the thumbs-up.

"So, let me get this straight – the missiles have now set off at the right time," marvelled Jed Jefferies.

"It seems so," said Tom.

"It seems so...or it is so?" asked JJ.

"Each missile is on course to hit the asteroid," answered Tom.

"And the asteroid...will it still be far enough away when they hit?" asked JJ.

There was a short silence, followed by a resounding, "Yes!"

"The window of tolerance was quite large, and we were set at its furthest extreme...now the missiles will hit quite a way in from that point, but it will still be safe and within tolerance!"

"How can it be that we were all set to hit this rock a day later than we are doing, but everything will still happen exactly as it should...only a day earlier? Also, if the system hadn't been tampered with, our missiles would have detonated a day too late...what is this – people, divine intervention!? I don't think so...because we are scientists at NASA. When this is over, I want a full evaluation of what has occurred here! As for now, I need you all to re-focus and deliver this mother fucking rock a present from NASA!"

With that, JJ strode out of the door and back into the office again, and said, "Did you call the President yet?"

"He has been in a meeting for hours."

"And you didn't break up the meeting to tell him the world is coming to an end?" quipped JJ.

"What do you have to be sounding so happy about? You have just sent the world's total arsenal into space on a wild goose chase!"

"No I haven't!" said JJ.

"What!?"

"It turned out to be a glitch in the system. I'm glad he was in a meeting... you would have sounded silly phoning him back!" laughed JJ.

"You mean...everything is...alright? The missiles...they are...alright??" His superior looked incredulous.

"As right as rain," said JJ, leaving the room. His boss just stared at where JJ had been standing, his mouth agape and his eyes glazed.

By now, Tamara had given up on a long, luxurious soak and was out of the bath and dressed again. She looked in her mirror at the perfection in its reflected glory. She smiled and disappeared, reappearing in the cabin of Paul Johnson and Dixie.

"Good evening, darlings…I feel a little overdressed," observed Tamara, sporting a customary raised eyebrow.

Johnson quickly covered himself and Dixie with a sheet.

"Do you ever use doors?" asked Johnson, blushing.

Dixie bowed her head, and was shocked at how Johnson spoke to the Listmaker.

"Doors are not fun – but appearing in front of naked people is," quipped Tamara.

"And what if we had been…well, you know, doing things?" asked Johnson.

"I would have joined in, darling…but enough of fun, there is plenty of time for that later, we need to talk now," said the impish Listmaker.

"Can we dress first?" asked Johnson.

"If you must – it's a shame Dixie has to dress, though," said Tamara sighing and rolling her eyes.

They both rose from the bed, Johnson quickly grabbing the sheet and running into the bathroom. Dixie, left totally naked, slowly walked up to Tamara and said, "How can I ever thank you for helping me get back to Paul?"

Tamara placed her elegant finger under Dixie's chin, lifted her face into the light, and said, "I will think of something, little one."

Tamara watched Dixie's slow exit, paying close attention to her posterior. As Dixie arrived at the door, she turned and said, "I hope so." Smiling sweetly, she disappeared into the bathroom.

Upon dressing, Dixie and Johnson re-joined Tamara out on the private terrace.

"We have had two close calls in a short time, and Dewhirst isn't very happy. There are two more boxes to retrieve…do you have your armour, Dixie?" asked Tamara.

"I do. It is in the wardrobe," answered Dixie.

"Excellent," said Tamara. "I am going to kit you out with some as well, Paul," she continued.

"Armour?" said the Chief Inspector. "Why armour?"

"Because we are taking a more direct route," answered Tamara.

"In what way?" asked Johnson.

"No more playacting. Just in, get the box, and out again...so, without the cover of one of your thoughts or dreams. That idea was just to make it easier for you to take part, and encourage you to do so," informed Tamara.

"That works for me! I just want this over with now, and to get back," said Johnson.

Tamara smiled and handed him a square twelve inch plain brown box that seemed to have no opening.

"What's this?" asked Johnson, not liking how the box felt in his hand.

"It's your armour," said Tamara.

"My armour is in a small box...that doesn't weigh anything? This will make me feel safe," was his sarcastic reply.

"Your sword is in there, too!" smiled Tamara.

"Now I know you're joking. I'm going into battle with a letter-opener. Thank you. I feel sooo protected now...I can't wait to leap into the fray!"

"Just wait until the box opens," said Tamara. Dixie smiled and held Paul Johnson's hand, gripping it tight, as Tamara disappeared.

"You will be much safer now, my love," comforted Dixie, as Johnson stood there holding Dixie with one hand and the skin-covered box in the other and an uncertain look on his face.

Morning had arrived, and the Jackson family were taking breakfast in the dining room.

"Gavin tells me you would like Alice as a bridesmaid, my dear," said Harriette to Sarah.

"Yes I do, because I only have one sister who I know will be too busy, and Alice is my only girlfriend who I would trust not to hurt me on my big day," said Sarah, finally stopping for air.

Harriette laughed and said, "It's fine child, I have no objections." Jarvis looked visibly shocked.

"That is wonderful, mum!" said Sarah as she leapt from the table and wrapped her arms around her soon-to-be mother-in-law. kissing her on the cheek, she ran out of the stuffy English dining room screaming, "Alice! Alice!"

Alice ran from the bedroom that she was tending to and arrived at the top of the stairs, wondering what was wrong. Sarah ran up the stairs two at a time, shouting at the top of her lungs. "Gavin's mam said yes! You are my bridesmaid!" The two girls hugged each other and Sarah was as happy as she could be.

Back in the sedate dining, room the three members of the Jackson family smiled at each other and carried on with their breakfast. Jarvis, as always, was on hand – but this time with the faint trace of a smile about his demeanour.

Paul and Dixie sat in their cabin; Johnson had been staring at the strange box ever since he had placed it on the table. It was as if it was drawing him in, somehow. Dixie removed his fixation with said box by gently kissing him on the cheek. He turned and smiled at her. The couple kissed passionately, but then heard a sound. On investigating, they found the noise to be the box opening. Johnson quickly started examining its contents. Now that it was open, he recognised this package as the open empty box found in the trash can at Lindale Mews at the start of the investigation that put John Smith in custody. With encouragement from Dixie, he very carefully placed his hand inside. His fingers wrapping tightly around a handle of some kind, with slight trepidation he withdrew the item from the box.

Just like Jeff Clarke, he was amazed at the size and weight of the sword that came from such a small box.

Checking over its enormous size he looked at Dixie and said, "How am I supposed to wield this?" Dixie just smiled and pointed at the armour that had replaced the box. "You wear that," she said.

"I think the Other Realm's tailor isn't very good at measuring," said Johnson

"Oh yes they are, that will fit you inch-perfect," answered Dixie. She opened her wardrobe door and pointed to her armour, saying, "Does that look like it fits me?" It was almost twice her size.

"How do I get in it – it looks like it is in one piece…" mused the disbelieving Chief Inspector.

"When I say now, just think that you are wearing the armour. Are you ready?" she said smiling.

"Yes," replied Johnson.

"Now."

The cabin disappeared from around them and they were both in the Other Realm.

"What's this?" asked Johnson.

"It is where you have been since you left the police station," said Dixie.

"So why do we both need armour now?" asked a slightly worried Johnson.

"The cover of your thoughts was the protective shield we used, but Atkinson discovered it, and you were almost killed," answered Dixie.

"Am I not on a cruise then?"

"No Paul, we have been here all the time," answered Dixie.

"So none of what has happened is real?"

"Just the box retrievals…and our making, and falling, in love," answered Dixie.

"Right then, that's ok – for a minute there, I was worried," said a relieved Chief Inspector.

"Shall we retrieve the last box here?" asked Dixie.

"There are two boxes left," corrected Johnson."

"No Paul, there is only one left in this realm," reaffirmed Dixie.

"In that case lead on," said Johnson.

Johnson and Dixie made their way through what looked like a high-walled valley. At the end of a long path was a stone mound protruding from the ground.

"You have to lift that huge stone, and remove the box from underneath," said Dixie.

Johnson lifted his arms and with a gripping motion began to try and move the rock with his mind. "It's ok Dixie...I am ahead of you... I have seen Star Wars," said Johnson through gritted teeth.

"What are you doing?" said Dixie

"M...mov...moving th...the r...rock!" huffed Johnson under great strain.

"You silly man," said Dixie, laughing. "You grab the other end of it, and we will lift it together," she continued

Johnson gave an embarrassed cough, and said, "I knew that, I was being light-hearted."

Dixie, still laughing, said, "What's Star Wars?"

"I don't want to talk about it," murmured the Chief Inspector.

As they drew near the rock, Dixie noticed a number of 'gatherer elementals'. She pointed them out to Johnson, saying, "These are the worst kind of elementals. They are less in number, but much stronger. They are used to reap the souls of murderers, and the like. What Atkinson and Dewhirst have done up to this point is reap souls, and each individual soul is then matched to an unborn child at one of three separate times during its development, and then reborn into a new life. When someone defiles our system by cutting short someone's allotted time, their cord is removed from the Realm of Death, and the gatherers get them. Needless to say, it might look like they have died peacefully, thinking they have gotten away free. But their soul has been devoured by the gatherers and that soul is not replaced."

"They sound troublesome," said Johnson.

"They will fight harder than elementals, but they have no allegiances to anyone – so when they realise there is no profit for them from this fight, they will all back off and run," informed Dixie.

"Ok...so, where is the trigger on this sword," asked Johnson.

Dixie gave him a look that said, "Not funny." She drew her sword and charged at the waiting gatherers. Johnson charged as well and waded into the most gruesome beings he had ever laid eyes upon.

Without noticing, his sword was lashing at these strange foes as if he was a professional sword fighter. Dixie too was matching everything that came at her. The gatherers were beginning to realise they were not able to get through their opponents' armour so they began to back off – first one by one, but then as more were seeing, what was happening they backed off in droves until all that was left were the two Warriors and the rock.

Night was beginning to fall in this weird realm as Dixie said, "Let's get the box and get out of here." Dixie and Johnson grabbed each end of the 12ft rock, lifted it, then casually threw it to the ground. In the hole under where the rock had stood guard was a square box containing Atkinson Junior's head. As soon as Johnson lifted it, the two Warriors and the box were transported back to the offices of Atkinson, Dewhirst & Smith.

The battle-weary couple were greeted by Tamara.

"You have done it! You retrieved all the body parts!" said Tamara.

"As I said to Dixie there is still one out there..." said Paul Johnson.

"You have been looking after it for us all the time," said Tamara.

"How so?" answered Johnson.

"Just come with me a moment," invited Tamara

Johnson and Dixie followed Tamara into a dark and musky old storage room filled with all manner of antiquities.

"What is that doing here?" asked Johnson, pointing at his own desk.

"I had it replaced with a little present for you. If you would care to open that particular drawer," asked Tamara pointing at the bottom one.

Johnson lifted the chain holding the key up and over his head and proceeded to unlock the drawer. To his amazement, in it was a small box, which he took out and gave to an eagerly-awaiting Tamara.

"The quest is fulfilled!" said Tamara triumphantly. Returning to the Reapers office, she placed the box on a large table that had been brought in by the Sunny Acres Mob for this very reason. She placed each severed part of Atkinson Junior's body in its rightful position on the altar-type table. There he lay, looking like the gruesome after-effect of a horrific rail accident. Tamara lovingly pushed each body part together, uttering strange words as each separate part was reunited.

A full hour passed by, whilst Paul Johnson and Dixie looked on in awe at Tamara's reanimation of her lifeless lover. With Atkinson's heart in her gentle hands, she placed it deep within the hole in his chest then started to squeeze and release it, squeeze and release it. She did this for thirteen minutes, muttering her incoherent incantation. She then removed her hands from his body, and the heart was pumping on its own. The hole in his chest closed, Johnson and Dixie, stared intensely at the goings on, moved closer. Tamara held Atkinson Junior's hand, and kissed his cheek. His deep blue eyes opened and he smiled at her.

In the Realm of Death, Atkinson Junior shouted to John Smith.

"I can feel the quickening! They have done it! I will see you on the other side, don't be late!" said Atkinson's apparition as he disappeared from John Smith's view.

In the Other Realm, the quickening was felt too. A rejuvenated Dewhirst walked into the chamber where Atkinson stood. He looked unmoved by the disturbance and said, "I see you have recovered from the little slap I gave you."

Dewhirst smirked at him and said, "No, I have recovered from you hitting me with all of your strength. I am recovered because you have the strength of a tired old man."

"We shall see," said Atkinson.

"Indeed we will, no sword, no armour, no chance. Your son is now stronger than he has ever been...stronger than you ever were" instructed Dewhirst.

"He will bow before, me and ask for mercy," screamed Atkinson.

"He will take your place as the Prophecy predicts – by going against the natural way of things, you are doing exactly what the greediest humans are doing on their planet. You cannot interfere with Nature...as you found out last time when you went against her. You cannot stop what is going to happen."

"I am Nature! When I decide to end things, they end!" said a defiant Atkinson.

"No, you are Death. You cannot make life, you can only end it," corrected Dewhirst. "When the Chosen One takes my place all my power and thoughts of my existence will be passed through me into him. When you feel the cold steel of your son's blade terminate your existence, your evil past will die with you, and thankfully a New Order will be in place," he continued.

"Be gone, Scribe! I want to look upon your face no more!" said Atkinson

"Be dead, Reaper...for you already are to me," answered Dewhirst.

Both Gods separated, and prepared for what was about to take place.

Chapter Ten

tkinson Junior sat up on the table and looked about him. Tamara brought him a robe to cover the fact that he was naked. Stepping down from the table, he placed his arms into the sleeves of the black silk robe that she was holding up for him. With no words spoken, he looked at Johnson and walked to him, extending his arm in friendship. Johnson pensively shook Atkinson Junior's hand.

"Thank you, Paul – do you mind me calling you Paul? As I seem to recall, on our last meeting you shot me, and things were not friendly between us. I do hope we can move on and maybe you could get to know the real me?" queried Atkinson Junior.

"Things have indeed moved on, and changed for the both of us. I have been informed you are not the monster you appeared to be, so, yes – I would like the chance to get to know you," answered the Chief Inspector.

Dixie had not said anything, because she was actually looking at the God Atkinson's son – and all the rumours about his existence, and his appearance, were true. She tried to hide herself behind Johnson, in the fear that even looking at him could be dangerous.

"And who do we have here?" asked Atkinson Junior, peering at Dixie.

"This is Dixie – she is a worker from our realm. We have her to thank for saving the quest," informed Tamara.

"Come forth, little one."

The raging Warrior of two hours ago was now a quivering wreck. She gingerly came from behind Johnson, and knelt on the ground, lowering her head.

"Please rise, Dixie. Now…how can I show my appreciation?" asked Atkinson.

Dixie tried to speak, but words eluded her tongue-tied mouth.

"She would like to be with Paul," said Tamara, coming to Dixie's aid.

"Become a human?!" said Atkinson.

"Yes, in a word," replied Tamara.

"I think you deserve a little better than that!" said Atkinson to Dixie, whilst looking at Tamara.

"Do you want this being, Paul?" asked Atkinson.

"She is everything I want," said Johnson.

"Do be clear about this – I can offer you anything your heart desires for the help you have given me."

"All I desire is Dixie," said Johnson calmly.

"Then welcome to the family! Don't worry, that strange feeling will soon pass," said Atkinson, as a wave of nausea took over Johnson.

"What's going on?" asked Johnson.

"Don't worry Paul, you will feel better soon," comforted Tamara.

Paul Johnson fell into Dixie's arms as he passed out.

"There you go, Dixie…he is an Immortal now, and yours forever," announced Atkinson.

At this point, John Smith returned from the Realm of Death. There before him, at the other end of the room, was Smith's master…his enemy…his friend. The two Reapers walked towards each other but as their hands almost touched, the office erupted in a whirlwind, throwing desks, chairs and occupants in all directions.

The two Reapers moved back from one another, acknowledging the fact that they could not be in the same place at the same time. Tamara and Dixie, still holding onto Paul Johnson, both stood back up, looking slightly windswept. Johnson returned to consciousness.

"Whatever happened?" he asked in a bewildered state.

Tamara explained that John Smith and Atkinson Junior had tried to shake hands...the effect of which had caused an internal storm.

Mr. Braithwaite and several of his colleagues then swiftly came into the room, and began clearing up the mess that had been caused, returning the office to its former pristine state. Paul Johnson was absolutely amazed to see that Mr. Braithwaite and his elderly posse appeared to be elementals. Tamara noticed his puzzled expression and said, "You can see them for what they are now, Paul. You will see many things differently now, with your new eyes."

"My new eyes?" replied Johnson.

"Yes, my friend. I have made you an Immortal," informed Atkinson Junior.

"But I don't want to be Immortal," said the ruffled Chief Inspector.

"I will not allow Dixie to become human. You said you wanted her. She is now yours," explained Atkinson.

Johnson looked thoughtful. Atkinson continued. "If I hadn't made you an Immortal, leaving Dixie out of the equation, how long do you think you would have lasted out there? You, my friend, are the human who brought my body parts back. My father hates humans in general, so you would have been terminated as soon as you walked out of this building."

Johnson thought some more, and quipped, "Putting it that way, I'm glad to be an Immortal."

Dixie placed her arms around Johnson and squeezed him tight.

"Tamara – I take it you can find work for Dixie within this building... and she doesn't have to return to her mundane work?" asked Atkinson.

"I certainly can! I can house them too – they can have Lindale Mews," said Tamara.

"I had almost forgotten about that place," said John Smith.

In the country, the weekend drew to a close. Gavin and Sarah bid their goodbyes. Harriette Jackson had decided to let Alice leave with her son and soon-to-be daughter-in-law to help Sarah prepare for her big day. The first stop on their way back was going to be at the new apartment.

Harriette and Donald sat back in their respective comfortable chairs and relaxed. After their weekend of entertaining Sarah, both of them looked like they had run a marathon.

Johnson and Dixie climbed the stairs to number 3 Lindale Mews. As they reached the door, Johnson hesitated and said, "I don't know if I want to be here after the carnage that took place."

"What carnage?" asked Dixie, as she opened the door to an immaculate re-designed apartment that was wall-to-wall luxury.

"On the other hand...maybe it will be okay," said Johnson, correcting his earlier statement. "When you said 'what carnage', did you mean you don't know what happened here...or is there something I'm not privy to?" continued Johnson.

"It would not do for a Chief Inspector to move into a murder scene, now would it?"

"Now you have lost me," he said.

At this point, the landlady appeared.

Dixie bowed her head, and Paul Johnson said with a hint of sarcasm, "Tamara! What a surprise! I haven't seen you in ages! What can we do for you?"

Tamara smiled and said, "Everything that has happened in this realm has been but a shadow whilst you have been away...also, everything about your and your late Superior's investigation no longer exists. The battle about to take place will be in a different realm, so as far as police records are concerned, none of this has taken place."

Johnson looked more puzzled than he had in days. On seeing this puzzled expression, Tamara said, "As far as everyone at the police station is concerned, everything about the case against John Smith and his lawyers has been removed...and you, my friend, have simply gone out to lunch."

"What about Scrivens?" said Johnson.

"There was never a Scrivens," answered Tamara.

"The problem with the volcano fissure?"

"That was simply Gavin, closing an old portal," answered Tamara.

"What about Jack, Sid and young Matt?" asked Johnson.

"Your old boss died of a heart attack...and the old newsman, a brain aneurysm. An unfortunate accident took the life of the young boy. It's all in Gavin's reports, on your new desk, waiting for you when you return from your lunch."

"So everything is back to how it was?"

"No... the earthquakes and the volcano happened...and the newspaper building did explode, killing many people...but everything else has been struck off the records, and the memories of everyone concerned. The Accountancy building still has the name Atkinson, Dewhirst & Smith – but hopefully, not for much longer," informed Tamara.

Tamara bid them a good afternoon, and her thoughts now turned to plans of her own. Dixie and Johnson looked about at what was going to be their home for a time – and liked what they saw.

John Smith and Atkinson Junior sat at either end of their office, discussing how the new Administration would work.

Tamara returned and said, "I have a date with Mr. Atkinson tonight, Mr. Smith...and you have a young man from the Coroner's office wanting to speak with you about investments...shall I send him in while I take Mr. Atkinson home?"

"Indeed! Please do, Tamara," said John.

On leaving the office arm-in-arm with Atkinson, Tamara said to the man waiting, "Please do go in."

"Mr. Harper! How nice to see you again!" greeted John.

As Tamara and Atkinson Junior arrived back at her apartment, all of her personal elementals were in the entrance hall, awaiting their arrival. As Atkinson Junior entered, they all lay face-down on the floor in his honour.

"They seem to have chosen their allegiances already," whispered Tamara into his ear.

Atkinson smiled and walked inside. The lounge had already been prepared – lights were dimmed, soft music playing and sweet-scented oils were warming by candlelight. The ambiance of love was heady in the room. Upon taking his coat and shedding hers, Tamara took hold of Atkinson's hand, and the couple sat on the enormous sofa and sipped vintage wine. All thoughts of the past and future battles melted away from their joined minds as they relaxed close to each other on the couch.

"you have no idea how many times I thought of this during my exile." said Atkinson softly whilst kissing Tamara's ear. He began to gently caress her neck, and her chin lifted in arousal. She gasped as he placed a kiss directly onto one of her erogenous zones... it was a kiss that he'd perfected upon Tamara's neck over the centuries of their amour. His chin caught her loosely-fitting strap, softly, but with just enough force to slip it off her porcelain-perfect shoulder. As the strap fell, the part of her top that was connected to it folded over, leaving a small triangle of its underside and revealing the upper part of her breast. She could take no more, and turned to kiss his waiting lips.

He accepted her kiss with passion. He had adored this being over many millennia, but this kiss was the most potent they had ever exchanged. Atkinson felt truly reborn. Their passion was the stuff legends are made of. He was glad just to be in this embrace – if nothing else happened on that night, he would be fully satisfied. This night, however, was far from over, as Tamara kicked off her high-heeled shoes and lay back in his lap. They gazed upon each other like two teenagers with the first expectation of love. Atkinson stroked his long fingers through her hair as he stared into her eyes. Tamara realised this was indeed her Atkinson of old. The tender, thoughtful God who had no interest in destruction, and the only one of the three who actually truly loved the humans.

"It seems so long since I've looked upon your beauty, Tamara; the Other Realm can play tricks upon your mind, and make time pass so slowly. Come my love, let's go upstairs," urged Atkinson.

Tamara rose and held her hand out to help Atkinson off the couch, and together they climbed the stairs to the bedroom. She turned around, taking hold of his other hand, coaxing him into the room. Tamara unbuttoned his shirt, took it from him and dropped it to the ground. After unbuckling his belt, she undid the catch on his trousers; they too fell to the floor and he stepped free of them, with a clear indication that many centuries of making love to the same person hadn't grown tiresome.

The sight of her lover naked only made her want him more. She removed her top, unzipped her skirt, and let it fall to the ground. After gracefully removing her knickers, the two of them embraced. Although in effect he was a masterful beast, he was as gentle as a lamb, as he lifted her up and walked to the bed. Laying her down, he began to kiss and caress her body, again hitting every erogenous zone she possessed. Her full satisfaction was all he could think of as he lavished all kinds of intimate pleasures upon her eagerly-awaiting body. He continued his loving foreplay until Tamara was ready to receive him. As if he was making love to a fragile fairy, he tenderly entered her, slowly easing his manhood in with soft, featherlike motions. Her groans of extreme pleasure echoed all through the apartment.

She writhed in ecstasy as her climactic moment approached. Atkinson, with the finesse of a ballet dancer, gently loved his woman to a place she had almost forgotten. She had been making love with a God, and part of his greatness was now rushing within her. Exhausted, she lay back on the bed. Atkinson held his lover's hand and kissed her lips. He looked deep into her eyes, which were welling with tears, and saw his own eyes reflected within them. Now, he truly felt he had returned...and this time...he was himself.

Back at the office, John Smith had droned on for an hour and a half about the financial ups and downs of stocks and shares when Tom Harper said to him, "Would you like to go for a drink?"

John Smith, realising he had let a part of his old character back into his life, and the poor man in front of him was about to expire of sheer boredom, said, "Um...yes...I think I would!"

Tom Harper smiled and said, "I can only do so much arithmetic in one go."

Both men laughed. Smith depressed the intercom button and said, "I take it I have no more appointments, Mr. Braithwaite?"

"You have an appointment..."

Mr. Braithwaite was stopped by Smith depressing the button once again.

"I take it I have no appointments, Mr. Braithwaite?"

"None at all, Sir, you are clear for the rest of the day," answered Braithwaite.

The two gentlemen left the old Tudor building and walked down the main street of town to the southern end of the road and into a little public house on their right-hand side. The pub was just in front of a railway bridge...it was, in fact, part of a long viaduct that dissected the city in two. The aptly-named pub was warm and inviting, and quite an eye-opener to both men.

It was a huge eye-opener to John Smith, because up until a year or so ago, he had led a very sheltered life. The pub was a revelation to Tom Harper, too, because his life had revolved around his work. Neither man had ever visited this part of town before. It wasn't too long before the two men realised fate had played a trump card, and delivered them into the 'Pink Quarter' of town – and one of its most welcoming establishments. After some normal chitchat...weather and that kind of thing...John Smith said, "I rather like this place." Tom agreed.

As the two men were talking, two extremely handsome young men came to where they were sitting, and one of them said, "Hi, Tom! I haven't seen you in here before. Who is your friend?

"Hello, Mike, I have never been here before. This is my friend John Smith. John, this is my colleague Mike, from the Pathology Dept."

"Hi John, this is my friend Mikey."

"Hello! This is quite a friendly place," observed John.

"This whole area is great!" replied Mikey.

The four men sat talking for a while, discussing different places, and different events held in this section of town. A scuffle then broke out at the bar...a group of small-minded thugs had managed to evade the door staff and were now demonstrating how 'manly' they were by picking on and heckling innocent individuals. They suddenly spied the four men sitting together at the table and made a beeline for them.

John Smith stood up and placed himself in front of the trouble-makers. All five of them laughed as they closed in on him. With movement the speed of which human eyes could not detect, he punched each one separately. The punch delivered the same effect as the impact of a steel bar. Then, at normal speed, he lightly slapped each one of them at the sides of their faces in a circular but comical fashion. These 'hard men' fell like a line of dominoes, unconscious and completely unawares, to the ground, just as the door staff ran in.

"What's happened 'ere?" asked the buff mountain of a doorman.

"They were rowdy...I was afraid they were going to cause trouble! I only gave them a little slap on the face..."

The doorman looked at the five six foot plus bruisers out cold on the floor and said, "If you don't tell me what happened, I'm going to call the police."

At this point, just as the hoodlums were beginning to come round, the girl behind the bar – trying desperately to stop laughing – shouted out, "That is exactly what happened! He gave them a girl slap and they all fell over!"

The whole bar erupted in laughter, and the embarrassed hard men were dragged out of the pub and thrown into the street, the bar staff and entire pub all the while roaring with laughter. The staff on the door told the gathered crowd of onlookers who had wandered over from 'Queen's Court' what had happened. They too joined in with howls of spontaneous laughter as the hard men had their 'Walk of Shame' out of the Pink Quarter of town.

"What a set of softies!" exclaimed Mike.

"Indeed!" answered Tom.

"That was amazing, John – you okay?" asked Mikey.

Realizing what he had just done, John Smith said, "I'm a little shaky...I...I think I should go home now, if you don't mind, Tom. That was rather frightening."

Turning to the two flamboyant gentlemen at his side, he said, "It was a pleasure meeting you both, Mike and Mikey!"

Turning back to Tom, he said, "I will be in touch," and then made his withdrawal.

As he left the pub, he felt adrenalin surging through his veins, and for the first time he began to understand his power. He had just rendered unconscious five large brutes with one light punch. On returning to his office, the Scroll for that night's work was laying on his desk. Whistling, he picked it up, twirled it in the air, and caught it like a famous gunslinger re-holstering his gun...then skipped through the open door into the Realm of Death.

JOHN PAUL BERNETT

Chapter Eleven

It was zero hour at NASA. All missiles were on course, to rendezvous with their target in one hour. Tension was high, as each individual controller was checking for any unforeseen problem in the final countdown to end this destructive threat to Humankind. Jed Jeffries' eyes were transfixed on his screen. The last three hours had been taken up by checks and re-checks, and here he was, in charge of a team of scientists and academics – the World's salvation resting on his shoulders.

His forehead was furrowed, as he kept going over the individual systems, still running checks. He had stopped smoking three years earlier...but a short trip to the cigarette vending machine in the corridor had put a stop to that. His ashtray already contained many stubs. He lit yet another one as he announced to his Controllers,

"I want a go or no-go for acquisition of target."

Each individual controller responded with a "Go flight!" or simple "Go!" But, some of the more flamboyant members of the team shouted "Lock and load!" or "Target acquired!" However they answered, he received a full count of 'go'.

Fitted to the last missile to be launched, that was set to trail all the others, was a high-resolution camera. This was their 'eye in the sky', and JJ gave the go-ahead for it to be switched on.

The first image was just a black screen, but then the screen flickered several times, and the first images of the Earth-saving armada were transmitted to the large screen at the front of Mission Control. Looking at the sheer size of the target was breath-taking, as one controller remarked, "I hope we have enough missiles."

"Let's just pray that we do," answered JJ.

"Controllers, may I have your attention, please? We are counting down and are at forty-five minutes to impact. All of the warheads are armed and are locked on target. We have done all we can do, ladies and gentlemen – it is now out of our hands."

Gavin and Sarah stood arm-in-arm on the rooftop balcony of their new penthouse apartment. In front of them could be seen the panoramic view of their town, and miles beyond.

"I hope everything stays like this," said Sarah.

"I'm sure it will, Sarah," comforted Gavin.

There was a ring of a bell as the private elevator door swished open. The occupant of the elevator was none other than Atkinson Junior in full figure. There was a second or two of uncomfortable silence – and then as before with Johnson, Atkinson held out his hand in friendship. The meeting that Sarah never wanted to happen was now taking place...only not how she had envisaged it. Atkinson Junior was proving to be a perfect gentleman; he seemed not to hold any hard feelings towards her for killing him...twice. In fact, things were so nice, they all sat in the lounge whilst Alice poured them a cup of tea.

"You have a servant?" enquired Atkinson.

"No. Alice is my friend," answered Sarah.

Standing up, Atkinson smiled and said, "Do forgive me, Alice...how presumptuous of me."

Alice just smiled.

"This is our friend and accountant, Mr. Atkinson," said Gavin to Alice.

"Very pleased to meet you, Sir," said Alice.

Sarah took Alice into the kitchen and said, "We have an afternoon of boring money-talk ahead of us...why don't you go out and explore...here is some money. Take the afternoon off, and have some fun."

Alice smiled sweetly and gave her friend a kiss on the cheek, then made for the elevator. Sarah returned to the lounge.

"So... what happens now you are back?" enquired Gavin.

Atkinson answered, "I must ready myself for battle...and be sure my small army is ready too...that is why I am here."

"You can count on both of us," answered Sarah.

Atkinson smiled and said, "I was hoping for that."

"When will it begin?" asked Gavin.

"The Prophecy is vague on that one...I enter my father's realm when the 'New Sun is on the wane' is the actual wording."

"New Sun?" repeated Sarah.

"That's what I mean...it doesn't really make sense how it is written down, but I do have an idea of what it might mean," said Atkinson, as he stood up.

"We shall see you later, then," said Sarah.

Atkinson smiled and left the room.

On entering the building of Atkinson, Dewhirst & Smith, he transformed into Warrior mode – an impressive sight to behold. A giant of a man clad in black chainmail – covered with body armour of the same colour with inlays of gold. His father's mighty sword rested in its scabbard at his side, his long black hair falling over his shoulders and down his back. All the clerks stood to attention with their heads bowed as he passed.

Stepping into the office, he said, "The time is nigh!"

Tamara instantly changed into her armour...and Jeff, looking slightly puzzled, appeared in his.

"Is this it? I don't know if I'm prepared...I'm not ready!" said a worried Jeff.

"You will be fine, Jeff. When you get the urge to join me, that will be me drawing you in. So when it happens, draw your sword and think 'Dewhirst'. Tamara...you know what you have to do," said Atkinson. Tamara nodded her head, once.

"Are you sure you don't want me in there with you?" asked John Smith.

"Know this, John Smith – should my father feel your presence within his chamber, he will kill you. He will do this so my new way will not work...the same applies to you, Jeff...come only when I call. Now...we wait for the sign," instructed Atkinson.

At NASA, the camera was now working perfectly, and the countdown showed five minutes on the clock; so far, all was going well. Only one missile had struck before its intended time, and all the rest were bearing down on a one-mile-square target area. Another glance at the clock, and it was three minutes to go. There was another flash on the camera as another solitary missile struck. To the surprise of the controllers watching, that blast threw out quite a lot of debris into space, the verbal count of thirty seconds began. Another few flashes burst out from the asteroid.

"Five, four, three..." flashes were now occurring all over the target area. "Two, one."

The asteroid turned into a mass of brilliant white light. Seconds later, large chunks of rock burst out in all directions – then came a rush of particles racing towards the camera – then the camera suddenly stopped recording the event.

Cameras were not needed to see the effect of the blast in the early evening sky. The explosion turned the side of the planet that was facing it back into full daylight. Although this strange phenomenon firstly put people into absolute panic mode, it sent Mission Control into euphoria. It wasn't long before news of the Planet-Saving Mission was passed through every news link throughout the world. People out in the streets saw the news on live city screens and in shop windows, whilst people indoors watched on their own TVs how close they had come to extinction. Little did they know Armageddon was still a threat...unless two unknown beings could fulfill an ancient prophecy.

After seeing the blast, Gavin and Sarah arrived in John Smith's office in full armour.

"We are here if needed," said Gavin.

As Atkinson watched the explosion light up the sky, he said, "To new beginnings – or to the end of all things."

Tamara took hold of his hand, and said, "All our hopes and love are with you – your father has no love for anything, so has no purpose to his fight. You fight to save Humankind, and our love – keep your heart safe...and your aim true."

Atkinson turned away from Tamara, pointing at Jeff with his mighty sword, and said, "When you feel me call, think 'Dewhirst', my brave boy. My friends, tonight sees the end of my father's reign... and I will be, truly, Atkinson."

On saying that name, he disappeared.

As soon as he had gone, Tamara summoned Dixie. Arriving instantaneously, she said with her head bowed, "I am here."

"Now – with the exception of John Smith, Dixie and Jeff – if I feel Atkinson needs our help, we join the fight."

"Why not me?" asked a puzzled Dixie.

"Because we have to keep the Reaper system running – Smith is the Reaper – you, Dixie, will take my place as Listmaker should I fall. Sarah, Gavin and I are the only ones strong enough, and all three of us are expendable," explained Tamara.

Gavin and Sarah stood, expressionless and ready to die for the cause.

Dixie bowed her head once more, and said, "As you command."

John Smith sat at his desk twirling a pencil around in his fingers, and said, "And if you three fall, what then? Will you be reanimated should Atkinson Junior slay his father?"

Tamara looked in the direction of Sarah and Gavin and said, "Other than the Reaping Sword, anything cut down by a weapon being wielded by Atkinson or Dewhirst is gone forever."

"And should Atkinson fall as well? What would the point of us still being here be, as Armageddon would swiftly follow his defeat?"

"That, dear John, sounds like the arrogance of the human within you…there is so much more to this world than its extremely short dominance by the homo sapiens. You will carry on reaping the dominant species. Everything else, including any stragglers of Humanity will, as has always been, be reaped by a different section of the company," informed Tamara.

"A different section?" asked John.

"It would be impossible for one Reaper to deal with every species on this planet. Each species has its own system that answers to Atkinson and Dewhirst. All life is equal, and dealt with in the same way. You are the most powerful Reaper, for yours are the dominant souls – not better or greater, just the Alpha ones of the moment. Sixty-five million years ago, the cords you would have been severing would have been connected to a Pterodactyl or a Brontosaurus," said Tamara.

"So I could be Reaping ants or seagulls next?" said Smith.

"You will Reap whatever the victorious Atkinson says you reap," instructed Tamara, ending a conversation she didn't really want to be in.

John Smith just raised an eyebrow, and went back to twiddling his pencil. Tamara sat down and tried to make mind contact with Atkinson Junior.

Atkinson Junior entered his father's domain. It was dark and uninviting. His pupils widened as his eyes reacted to the lack of light. His first sight was not his father…but Dewhirst.

"My fight is not with you, Dewhirst – I fight with Atkinson," said Atkinson Junior.

"Your father fears that which is prophesied...I do not. I will bring my replacement straight to me when you call him," said Dewhirst.

"Then I am forever in your debt. Now, please stand down and let me pass," said Atkinson Junior, bowing his head in respect of this old, and very tired Deity.

Dewhirst did as he was bid, and Atkinson Junior walked towards his destiny.

JOHN PAUL BERNETT

Chapter Twelve

The son entered his father's lair...it was dank, uninviting, and oozed his father's hatred of all things. A lesser being would have felt the weight of its intimidation, but the son's mind was transfixed on its purpose and did not notice the unwelcoming ambiance. He drew his sword and called his father's name in their own tongue...a language no human ear could ever understand, nor mouth could ever speak. He remembered in days long gone looking upon this powerful instrument of destruction in his hand, even as a child hearing his father say, "Look upon it, but know you this – your hand will never wield its power."

The weapon he drew was the sword that has been depicted on many an artist's canvas – as that of the sword of the Apocalyptical horse-rider 'War'. His expression showed no emotion...just a cold desire in his stare. Unhitching the cloak from his shoulders, it fell to the ground, and he thought *'That's one thing that you have wrong, father...ready yourself to be wrong again.'* The son was ready both mentally and physically, for the father...or the son's...final battle.

At NASA, the Hubble telescope relayed the images Jed Jeffries wanted to see. The asteroid not only had its trajectory altered, it had been completely destroyed...and trillions of small particles had been blasted out into the Solar System, none of them large enough to be of any worry. Champagne corks popped, and a party spirit replaced the furrowed foreheads and sweaty palms in Mission Control. This time, the message had gotten through to the President of the United States of America, and been relayed across the unsuspecting world.

The offices of Atkinson, Dewhirst & Smith looked surreal, with five battle-ready Warriors pacing about the place – and the Grim Reaper sitting at his desk, still twiddling his pencil. Tamara sat at her desk, concentrating on the mind link she had with Atkinson Junior. She was being careful to keep the channel one way, so her thoughts would not distract him.

"At the first sign of trouble, we will join him," said Tamara, looking at Gavin and Sarah.

"Why did we not go with him?" enquired Gavin.

"I wondered that too…" agreed Sarah.

Tamara smiled at her sister and said, "You have a habit of getting the killer blow in, young lady, and the Prophecy clearly states that Atkinson Junior – not 'Slabgirl' – will strike the fatal blow."

This brought a ripple of laughter and some much-needed ease to the tense group of warriors.

"So…you've come to face me, boy…" said the father.

"I am here to kill you," retorted the Son.

"But you have stolen my sword…how am I supposed to fight you with no weapon?" hissed the father.

"You have many swords – pick your best one and face me."

"Oh, but I am facing you, boy, can you not see me?"

"I expected this…so I borrowed something of yours from Smith before I left," said Atkinson Junior, as he placed the cloak of invisibility over his head. As he put it on, he twisted around 180 degrees.

"Just as I expected – you would have your blade at my back, you coward!" said the Son.

With the swish of a sword, his father's new sword was knocked away from its thrust. The two beings both removed their cloaks.

"So...you come here to dethrone your father."

"As I have already said, I am here to kill you."

"Why not kill Dewhirst, and take his place? We could work together...father and son."

"Enough of this!" said the son, lifting his weapon to strike...but the father had stalled him enough for a multitude of elementals to pounce upon him from behind.

One hundred elementals kicked and gouged at him as he lay on the ground. Laughing, the father raised his sword to kill his struggling son.

"This was all too easy..." the father smiled.

As his father's sword descended, a flash of steel and sparks sent it back in an upwards direction as Sarah's blade blocked its progress. She fought Atkinson back as his son released himself from the grips of the elementals. As Atkinson Junior regained his freedom, his father knocked the sword from Sarah's hands. As his blade came down upon her, Atkinson Junior pushed her to one side, repelling the death blow with his own blade. Clashes, sparks and thunderous sounds were emitted by both blades, as the father extended blow after blow upon his son's defensive sword.

The son repelled a further onslaught, then began to attack his father again. Smashing his blade again and again against his father's sword, he was beginning to overpower him, as Sarah regained her composure and was back on her feet. Atkinson saw this, and leapt in front of her. His son took this opportunity to deliver the first real killer blow on his father with a lightning-fast thrust into his heart...but the Father was ready for this, and moved out of the sword's way, leaving the blade to pierce Sarah in the heart instead. She screamed out in pain and gave Atkinson Junior a disbelieving glance...and died on the end of his Father's sword that he wielded.

In the office, Gavin cried out, "Sarah!"
Tamara said, "I must go…" and then disappeared.

The son retracted his weapon from his fallen Warrior's chest. She fell to the ground as he rushed towards his waiting father, who parried his every strike. The death of Sarah had given the father the edge he needed, and now had his Son on the defensive again. The ground shook with each repeated blow, which would deafen any human ear, and sparks illuminated the darkness as daylight raining down upon the son – to the sound of laughter from his father.

Tamara reappeared in a forest in a different realm, near the cottage where she and Sarah were born, and on the grass nearby lay her naked, slain sister. Moving over to her, Tamara kissed her forehead, then stroked her wound gently with her fingers. Sarah's eyes opened.

"Where am I?" she said in wonder.
"Take a look around you…" whispered Tamara.
"I'm home! Am I…dead?" asked Sarah.
"You were my little one, you went into battle whilst Atkinson was still strong," informed her elder sister.
"He needed my help…I had to go."
"And you were strong, and did your duty."
"But you said I couldn't come back if I was killed there…"
"I said only Atkinson's blade could kill you…"
"But it was his sword."
"Indeed it was, little one, but it wasn't him that wielded it," said Tamara.

Sarah looked down at her chest and saw a gold scar between her breasts, and said, "I'm alive! And you saved me!"

She placed her arms around her sister's neck and hugged her with all her might, tears streaming down her cheeks.

"Come now little one…we had better go back. If I was you though, I would think 'armour' first."

Sarah looked down at her naked body and giggled.

When they returned to the office, Gavin wasn't there.

"Where's Gavin?" asked Tamara.

"He disappeared shortly after you did," said Dixie.

"Oh, god. John – I need you to go into the Realm of Death to block it from Atkinson…I won't be long," said Tamara, as she disappeared again.

John instantly went through the door, leaving Dixie, Sarah and Jeff in the room.

In the Other Realm, the battle was now between the God Atkinson, his son and the Sentinel. Still, the father was holding both Warriors with some ease. Tamara drew her sword and joined the fray, shouting to the Sentinel, "Think 'Sarah'!"

Instantly, he disappeared and arrived back in the office, his sword raised and an angry expression on his face. On seeing Sarah, he dropped his sword, picked her up and twirled her around, screaming her name.

"I thought I had lost you forever!" said Gavin with tears in his eyes.

Sarah just smiled, placed her hands on his cheeks, and kissed him.

Tamara's sword gave Atkinson Junior some respite from his father's onslaught, as the Listmaker now took up the fight with hate in her eyes for the being she had always despised. Her strength was holding the father back, and the son had now recovered. He shouted, "Tamara! Office!"

Tamara disappeared, rejoining her brood back at Atkinson, Dewhirst & Smith.

Sitting back in her chair, she caught her breath, and said, "Please, no more going back in there until called to do so."

Gavin and Sarah looked like a couple of children who had just been given a good telling-off.

The father was now beginning to feel the weight of the attack from his rejuvenated son. This time, it was his turn to parry thrust after thrust from Atkinson Junior's blade. Blood was clearly visible now on both blades, as the son kept up his onslaught upon his father. Thinking his son was gaining the upper hand, Atkinson called upon a flock of gatherers, who came bursting into the room like a pack of rabid dogs.

The father laughed as the gatherers began biting at his son's arms and legs, rendering him, once again, weakened. His laughter could be heard throughout his domain...until the top half of a gatherer hit him fully in the face. His laughter stopped abruptly as he watched Tamara, Sarah and Gavin carve them all to pieces. Enraged, he ran at the group of beings, screaming...but all three had returned to safety before he arrived. The son, although bleeding from gashes delivered by the gatherers, advanced once more, sending long streaks of sparks from his father's blade...but still...Atkinson matched everything that his son could throw at him.

Dewhirst then entered the chamber in full regalia. He leaned on the wall, his arms crossed...watching the battle.

"So, you are just going to stand there and watch this upstart try to take my place?!" yelled Atkinson Senior.

"As the Prophecy predicts," answered Dewhirst.

"So...you won't fight...you'll just let that human infant take the place of the Great Dewhirst?" said Atkinson Senior as he looked aghast.

Dewhirst nodded and said, "Yes."

"You are premature with your surrender – I am about to finish my son off, and I will make sure your little pretender dies with him," snarled Atkinson.

Although the fight was still going on, the son was visibly tired – the horrendous wounds caused by the gatherers, and the elementals before them, had taken their toll. The thrusts of his sword began to lose their ferocity.

Back in the office, Tamara stood and said, "Something is not right...Atkinson has made it so his son's wounds won't heal...he is dying we must help!"

All but Dixie and Clarke disappeared, arriving in the Other Realm to see Atkinson holding his son by his hair, his sword readying for its final sweep to remove his head. Tamara screamed, "Noooo!" as the sword bore down on its target.

Within that very moment, John Smith burst from the Realm of Death, and with his Reaping Sword sliced off Atkinson's arm, which fell to the ground still clasping the sword. With his last ounce of strength, Atkinson Junior released himself from his father's grip and shouted, "Jeff!!!"

Instantly the boy appeared in front of Dewhirst, and with one loud shout of, "Now!" the son thrust his mighty sword into the cold heart of his father. Dewhirst, sensing Jeff's slight hesitation, walked onto his blade. As he did, he looked into Jeff's eyes and smiled. The sword deep within him was ablaze, with flashes of light emanating from it as the old God's thoughts – and power – passed through the weapon and into the being holding it.

Simultaneously, the father looked upon the son with disbelieving eyes, again with flashing lights glowing from the sword that the new Atkinson was holding. All of the power – but none of the thoughts of the slain beast – passed through it. Atkinson Senior and Dewhirst were gone. Long live Atkinson, Smith and Clarke!

The power surging through Atkinson and Clarke felt like electricity passing through their bodies. Atkinson's new regime could truly begin, and Jeff now had the experience of a thousand millennia passed onto him.

Looking about, Jeff said, "I think I will take a look at my new office," as he walked towards the Scribe's chamber.

Atkinson looked at Tamara, Sarah and Gavin and said, "Thank you all for your help." Turning to John Smith he placed his masculine arms around him, saying, "Again, I am in your debt...what can I do for you?"

"You can let me finish my Administration, now I have learned to have fun," said Smith.

"Of course you can. But being locked down here for years at a time is what changed my father from the great Reaper he was into the monster he became...so that will be my first change. As of this day, we can now be in the same place at the same time. That way, none of the three of us will ever get stir crazy," said Atkinson.

At that point, he drew Dixie into his Realm. She bowed upon her arrival.

"Your new position, Dixie, is Listmaker to Reaper Smith. That way, Tamara gets time off, and can spend it with me here, whilst I am with Jeff. You will spend twenty-five years at the desk, and then twenty-five years at rest. I'm sure your husband-to-be will approve, as you still get to spend time with him as an ordinary couple, then spend twenty-five years on holiday doing whatever pleases you."

Dixie was speechless, and tears welled up in her eyes.

Atkinson continued. "John Smith, I am and always will be in your debt. You are a true friend, and I am honoured to share in this friendship. Now...as we all can be together in the same place, I suggest we reconvene at the wedding," he said, smiling.

Gavin and Sarah smiled. Sarah put her arms around Atkinson and kissed him on the cheek; Gavin shook his hand.

"Now Jeff...I think you and I should get to know each other! Who is this pretty girl?" Atkinson beamed.

"This is Cindy...my prize for accepting the position."

Atkinson put his arms around the both of them and said, "How wonderful! Let's check your new domain."

The rest regrouped back at the offices of Atkinson, Smith and Clarke in normal attire. Mr. Braithwaite had already iced the celebratory champagne. Upon the realisation and grandeur of what had just unfolded, they all felt a sense of relief and euphoria at the same time.

"A toast," said Mr. Braithwaite, "To Atkinson."

The clinking sound of touching glasses brought this particular 'spanner in the works' of the real Reaper System to a satisfactory conclusion.

Chief Inspector Paul Johnson returned to the police station, after what had seemed a very long lunch.

"Good afternoon, Sir! Did you and Dixie enjoy your lunch?" asked Glenn Simpson the Desk Sergeant.

"Indeed we did!" said Johnson with a smile.

"Incredible what those chaps at NASA have done...you know...saving the planet and all that."

"I know...we are all indebted to them," said one of the unsung heroes that had actually saved the planet.

JOHN PAUL BERNETT

Epilogue

The Wedding

The Jackson country house looked beautiful in the midday sun. The bunting adorning the building's fascia was joyous. The marquee at the back of the house looked just as spectacular, with balloons and trimmings all around its massive structure. Jarvis was instructing the work force of the catering company as to precisely where, and how, everything should be placed on the tables.

Inside the house, Donald Jackson was complaining about his ill-fitting morning suit, tugging at the jacket, whilst Mrs. Jarvis was attempting to land the largest hat she had ever seen on the head of Mrs. Jackson.

"That hat looks bloody ridiculous!" said Donald to his wife, still trying to fasten his jacket.

"Be quiet, you silly old man! You know nothing of style!" retorted Harriette, in her custom-made, two-piece, pink silk suit, with matching handbag and shoes.

In the next room, Alice had her hair tied up and held in position with mock pearls and diamantes. Similar jewels adorned her bridesmaid's dress. She looked beautiful, as she attended the blushing bride.

"It's almost time, Sarah!" said Alice.

"I have no one to give me away," answered Sarah, a tear almost spoiling her makeup.

Alice quickly wiped the incriminating tear away, saying, "I don't understand – I assumed the elegant, tall gentleman waiting in the drawing room was here for that very reason."

Sarah looked upon her with puzzled eyes, and then ran out of the room and down the stairs. There, standing in the drawing room, was an absolute Adonis. Clad in black, his long black hair was tied into a ponytail, held by a black silk ribbon. His long bespoke coat, a masterpiece of tailoring, with its brocade cloth and Highwayman style, looked magnificent. Everything about his posture oozed importance. He opened his arms wide, and said, "I thought since you have killed me twice, and I have only killed you once, you owe me one. I also thought you giving me the honour of giving you away will just about even things up between us."

Sarah ran into Atkinson's arms and exclaimed, "My day is complete now!"

"Ahem...no it isn't, young lady," came a voice from behind her.

She turned and ran to her sister, who was dressed exactly like Alice.

"It is, now your Chief Bridesmaid is here," said Tamara, with a raised eyebrow.

Sarah hugged her tightly, saying, "Thank you! thank you!"

"It just so happened I had this Saturday off – oh – and all the other Saturdays for the next twenty-four years."

Gavin's parents arrived in the drawing room. "Quick brandy, anyone?" said Donald.

"Donald Jackson! Put that bottle down!" said a voice from underneath a very large pink hat.

"Sorry old girl, just steadying the nerves, you know."

"Really..." tutted Harriette.

Jarvis entered the room and announced quite stiffly, "The wedding vehicles have arrived, Madam..."

Harriette instantly turned into a Sergeant Major, and marched everyone outside. Jarvis opened the door to the first Rolls Royce, and helped Harriette and Donald into the rear seats. Into the last Rolls he helped Sarah and Atkinson. Then, into the middle one, he assisted Tamara and Alice. Then he held out his hand to his wife, helping her inside, and lastly boarded himself. The motorcade slowly left the house for its one and a half mile journey to the church.

Earlier, Gavin Jackson and his best man Hugo Thornton-Ellis had travelled the same route. They had left whilst the bridal party were still upstairs. Stepping out of the vehicle, Gavin noticed a small crowd of people outside the church yard. He smiled at them, and bid them all a good day. As they walked into the church, Gavin whispered, "I wonder who those people are?"

In a rather posh voice, Hugo answered, "I suspect they are locals who just turn out on nice days like this to see the bride."

This was good enough for Gavin, as he walked down the aisle with his best man. In the pews to his right sat the well-to-do people in suits from his parents' side of the family; aunties, uncles...endless cousins, nephews and nieces...and friends. On the left-hand side were Sarah's friends in an array of purple and black. These fascinating people had wonderfully-coloured hairstyles, and wore all manner of Gothic, Victorian, Edwardian dress and Punk attire. They all sat waiting for the arrival of their friend, Slabgirl, every single one of them whispering about what the bride might wear.

Sitting in the front pews were John Smith, Tom Harper, Dixie, Chief Inspector Paul Johnson, Jeff, and Cindy. The stage was set and all they needed now was the bride.

Outside, the small crowd had grown into quite a large one as the motorcade reached its happy destination.
Harriette and Donald exited their car first, and the celebrated wedding photographer from Leeds, Mr Allan Ridsdale was capturing the event. Then, it was Sarah and Atkinson's turn to be caught on film with her bridesmaids.

When Mr. Ridsdale had finished his work, the bridal party entered the church, and the young organist played the Bridal March.

With the exception of Gavin, all heads turned to watch the entrance of the bride. With gasps from Gavin's side and cheers and clapping from Sarah's side, she began her triumphant march towards her man. As she came down the aisle she saw her friends; Sarah – with the bright orange hair, Wednesday and JP, Jack and Paul (who were to be the DJs later), Laura, Daz, Stuart and little Sarah. Her Bestie Sarah Fae, with her long pink and blonde dreads, smiled as she went past, as did her husband Shane in full military dress.

"You are not going to believe this..." said Hugo Thingy Thingy as Sarah advanced towards Gavin.

As she arrived at his side, Gavin looked at his wife-to-be. The vision he saw took his breath away. Sarah had not done what his family expected. She had not done what her friends expected. Her seamstress came from the Other Realm. Sarah was adorned in a beautiful Fairy Queen outfit, with real wings that fluttered when she walked. Her dress was gossamer...with a thousand glints of green glittering through the many layers of this magical, sparkling fabric. Upon her head was a ring of flowers with dragonflies circling it. Her bouquet was made of hundreds of butterflies with quivering wings. Her train was long and flowing, made from a similar fabric. It was held by her two bridesmaids, and at her side stood a magnificent God.

The vicar began the ceremony of the wedding of Gavin and Sarah. Within thirty minutes, they were married, and emerging from the church doorway.

Confetti rained down upon them as they came into the sunlight. The crowd standing outside the gates had grown a thousand fold. After the finishing photographs had been taken, the happy couple climbed into the horse-drawn carriage, ready to start their way back to the house. Sarah stood up, turned her back to the guests, and threw her bouquet over her head. With a gasp from the crowd, all of the butterflies flew apart, then away. The handle, with a small bunch of flowers attached, landed in Dixie's hands. Dixie turned and kissed Paul. Sarah sat back down, and the horse pulled away from the church. As the couple looked down the road, they saw it was lined on both sides with complete strangers...thousands of people they didn't know had journeyed to that spot from all over the world...and didn't know why. All they knew was they had to be there...and be thankful to the couple going by.

As the guests waved them off, two young Goths came up to Atkinson. He looked down upon them and smiled.

"Can I help you?" he asked.

One of them said, "We know who you are...thank you, for saving us."

Atkinson thought back to a dark time...and a pepperoni pizza with extra mushrooms.

As they were being pulled along the crowd-lined road, Sarah placed her lips onto Gavin's ear and said in a whisper, "I have a wedding gift for you...I am pregnant. There is a tiny Sentinel growing inside of me..."

Gavin's eyes widened with excitement. He kissed his bride, but was almost lost for words.

"I wonder what such a baby will be like?" asked Sarah.

"We all shall have to wait and see." replied a very happy Groom.

The End
of the beginning

JOHN PAUL BERNETT

John Paul Bernett

E-mail jonno41@hotmail.com

Twitter www.twitter.com/JPBernett

Facebook www.facebook.com/JPBernett

JOHN PAUL BERNETT

John Paul Bernett

Be Happy

www.ingramcontent.com/pod-product-compliance
Lightning Source LLC
Chambersburg PA
CBHW060926180626
46817CB00004B/1411